FORSAKEN

Fae

BOOK THREE

Other books by R. A. Steffan

FORSAKEN

Fae

BOOK THREE

R. A. STEFFAN

Forsaken Fae: Book Three

ISBN: 978-1-955073-04-2 (paperback)

For information, contact the author at
http://www.rasteffan.com/contact/

Cover art by Deranged Doctor Design

First Edition: July 2021

Author's Note

This book contains adult material. It is intended for a mature audience.

Table of Contents

ONE

"Perhaps, in the end, it does not matter." The quiet words, spoken against the side of Len's neck, broke the preternatural stillness inside the hollow tree trunk where he and Albigard were being held prisoner.

Len's knees were screaming in protest after an hour or more spent awkwardly hunched around Albigard's trembling body. They'd been dumped here after their audience with the Fae Court had gone spectacularly wrong, culminating in Albigard lying to his father to prevent Len from being used as a hostage against him.

Apparently, the Fae prohibition against intentionally misleading another was more than just some strange cultural code of conduct. When Oren had questioned him, Albigard insisted dismissively that Len was of no importance to him, and held no value beyond his potential utility in containing the Wild Hunt. The moment the lie had passed his lips, Albigard lost his magic—leaving him teetering on the verge of physical and emotional shock. He'd barely managed to hold himself together long enough for the guards to portal them back to this cell and restrain him against the wall with magical bonds.

Len had managed to calm him down enough to pry out of him exactly what had happened. Since then, he'd been plastered to Albigard's side as tightly as he could manage... at a loss for what to do beyond holding him.

A Fae who intentionally misleads another is no longer Fae, Albigard had told him ages ago, when this mess had first started. Len had dismissed the words as some kind of stupid, old-fashioned proverb.

And—*hey!* Look where *that* had gotten him.

"Of course it matters," Len told him, refusing to move or let go despite his imminent need for knee replacement surgery. "I told you. We'll figure something out."

The irony of spouting such blatant bullshit under the circumstances wasn't lost on him. For one thing, Len had absolutely no idea how to reverse the loss of a Fae's magic caused by lying. And for another, Albigard wasn't wrong. If he ended up being sacrificed to the Hunt, whether or not he had magic when he died wouldn't make a whole lot of difference to the end result.

Yet somehow, saying *yeah, you're probably right about that* seemed like a dick move. Call it human cultural conditioning, but Len couldn't bring himself to do it.

"What did your dad mean when he said you were keeping pets again?" he asked instead, because while that was probably a horrible choice of conversational gambit as well, it was still better than the alternative.

Albigard sagged in Len's grip, as much as the invisible force pinning him to the wall allowed, anyway.

"Over the centuries, I have occasionally taken humans as vassals for various reasons," he said.

"Yeah," Len replied. "I'd kind of noticed."

Fae held alarming amounts of power over human beings, simply by virtue of their magic. Human myths held repeated warnings against accepting gifts from the fair folk—and with good reason. As Len had learned firsthand, doing so gave the Fae in question a connection to your soul. Depending on their particular abilities, they could use that connection to track you, or to draw power from you to bolster their own.

Albigard already held such connections with both Zorah Bright and Vonnie Morgan—the first, a vampire who was currently deceased, and the second, a human with natural magic of her own. When Len had voluntarily accepted a gift from Albigard, it had been because that was the only way to power their escape from the Wild Hunt after they'd been cornered inside a dead pocket realm.

To date, Albigard hadn't abused the bond or given Len cause to regret the decision. Of course, that might have had something to do with the fact that Len was an untrained necromancer, and utilizing the animus that he attracted from the dying was physical agony for a Fae who normally depended on living things for power. But even so—

"I don't get the impression that collecting human vassals is all that unusual for your people,"

Len said. "So that still doesn't really explain the 'pet' remark."

"It is not unusual, no," Albigard agreed. "However, I have generally resisted using those humans as mindless foot-soldiers to increase my status and power on Earth. That part... is, in fact, somewhat unusual."

Len's stomach twisted as he took the words on board. He'd seen human military commanders grovel in front of Unseelie operatives who secretly pulled the strings of power on Earth. He'd felt the pull of Fae influence on his own thoughts, even though his necromancy gave him a measure of resistance to Fae magic.

"Oh," he said. "Right."

So, apparently Oren considered the fact that Albigard didn't make a habit of using controlled human slaves as literal or metaphorical cannon fodder to be a source of contempt. The level of hatred Len was coming to feel for Albigard's father probably should have alarmed him, since he wasn't normally a hateful kind of person. Unfortunately, there were so many other things alarming Len these days that his fervent desire to pound Oren into the dirt was buried pretty far down the list right now.

"Quite," Albigard said faintly.

"Well, for what it's worth," Len told him, "I'm rather appreciative of your moral stance on the subject, under the circumstances."

Albigard let out a harsh, stifled noise. "It's a moot point now, anyway. With my magic gone, you're as free as any human can be... while incarcerated in a jail cell in Dhuinne, at any rate."

"And you're still really bad at reassurance," Len retorted. "But I'm keeping your stupid hair tie anyway, so there."

Albigard's gift—a little strip of cotton fabric torn from the prisoner's garb he'd been wearing— had been clenched in Len's fist when the Fae portaled them out of the dead pocket realm, whisking them away to safety in Chicago. Later, he'd stuffed it in the pocket of his jeans without giving the action too much thought. A meaningless gesture, probably—but it was still there, sharing space with the energy bars Vonnie had pressed on him when he and Albigard had left Earth and traveled through the gateway to the Fae realm.

Before Albigard could come up with any sort of reply to Len's outburst of sentimentality, a large patch of the tree-trunk wall to their right began to glow orange.

"What the *hell*?" Len breathed, instinctively turning to place his body between the unknown danger and the helpless man behind him. A subsonic vibration hummed through the air, setting Len's teeth on edge.

"I do not know," Albigard replied, in the tone of someone who was already running close to capacity when it came to unexpected plot twists.

Len pressed his back against Albigard's front as the vibration became bone rattling, steadying himself with a palm against the rough surface of the wall. The wood shuddered and creaked beneath his hand. Meanwhile, the glow intensified until it was hard to look at, and he was forced to turn his face away.

A second later, the affected section of the tree trunk exploded inward, peppering them with bits of wood. Normally, Len would have yelped in shock, but at this point his shock receptors seemed to be pretty thoroughly burned out. When a figure in silhouette stepped through the brand new, person-sized hole in the side of the tree, Len wasn't nearly as surprised as he should have been to recognize the dreadlocked female Fae who'd slipped out of the Court hearing just as he and Albigard were being dragged away.

"Oh," he said stupidly. "It's you. Um... hello."

A second, taller figure stepped through the gap—male, but wearing the same kind of rough, primitive clothing as the woman. The pair was the polar opposite of the other bejeweled and buttoned-up Fae Len had seen since arriving here. They looked wild. Uncivilized.

The woman gave Albigard a quick onceover, not sparing Len much more than a fleeting glance.

"He's bound," she said to her companion. "Free him quickly; guards will be coming."

"Wait—you're busting us out of here?" Len asked. "Why?"

"Stand aside, human," said the male Fae.

Len didn't move from his protective crouch. "Albigard?" he asked. "It's your call. Yes or no?"

"I have no doubt that if you do not move out of the way voluntarily, they will remove you by force," Albigard replied dryly. "And in fairness,

I'm not certain our circumstances can really get any worse than they currently are."

Len winced. "You know, one of these days you and I need to have a talk about the concept of tempting fate." Even so, he moved out of the way beneath the male Fae's severe look before making another attempt to get information. "At least tell us who you are before you kidnap us?"

The male crouched, running his hands over the space a few inches from Albigard's body. After a few moments of concentration, he clapped one hand to Albigard's forehead and the other to his chest. Coils of light flared across Albigard's body. He jerked as though he'd been shocked, and slumped forward when the light disappeared — free of his bonds.

Well... free except for the iron collar and shackles, anyway.

Len hurried to catch him before he could land face-first in the dirt. He helped Albigard stagger to his feet, even though Len's own legs weren't feeling much steadier than his companion's appeared to be.

"Seriously," Len said. "Answer the question, damn it! *Who are you*?"

The woman gave him a tight smile that came nowhere near her eyes.

"We are the Forsaken," she said. "And we must leave before guards descend on the Dead Forest in force."

8

TWO

Len gaped at her, aware that Albigard was wearing an identical open-mouthed expression as Len steadied him with a hand around his upper arm.

"Move," hissed the male Fae. Swirls of fiery magic twisted around his raised right hand.

Len snapped his jaw shut and moved, dragging Albigard along with him. Before they'd completed their awkward sideways shuffle through the shattered hole in the tree trunk, the sound of crackling flames heralded multiple Fae portals opening around them. There were more of the ragged Forsaken arrayed outside, and they turned toward the incoming threats with clutched weapons and hands sparking magic, ready to cast.

Guards poured through the open portals, and suddenly blasts of magic were flying all around them. Len's breath caught in his throat as he debated lunging for cover inside the tree they'd just escaped — but there were noises of battle coming from that direction, too.

An invisible force slammed into the thick bark inches from Albigard's head. Before Len could properly start to panic, the woman with the moss-colored hair slipped past them and threw up a hand in a blocking gesture. A wavering glow shimmered into existence in front of them, bolts of magic impacting it and sizzling into uselessness as she strained to hold the barrier steady.

Len chanced a look over his shoulder, trying to see what was happening inside the destroyed tree cell, since there was nothing protecting them against an attack coming from that direction. A flash of light burned his retinas and a guard fell through the opening with a grunt. Next to him, Albigard jerked his arm free of Len's hold and pulled a dagger from the female Forsaken's belt—hunching awkwardly to accommodate the chains shackling his wrists to the iron collar encircling his neck.

He fell to his knees next to the writhing guard and plunged the blade through the left fifth intercostal gap near the man's mid-clavicular line. Len's chest jolted as though *he* were the one who'd just been knifed through the heart—but before his brain could settle on some kind of a coherent reaction to the fact that Albigard had murdered someone right in front of him, a whoosh of icy cold power exploded outward from the dying guard and settled around Len's shoulders like a cloak of lead.

He staggered, catching himself clumsily against the side of the tree—the breath catching in his lungs. "*Fuck,*" he choked, as Albigard looked up with hard green eyes to gauge his reaction.

A spatter of crimson blood painted one perfect cheekbone, looming in Len's wavering vision as the chill of the Fae guard's death animus sank beneath Len's skin and disappeared.

He'd barely recovered his equilibrium when a second wave hit him, an instant before a headless body fell across the first guard's corpse like a sack of potatoes, with blood pouring from the stump of its neck. Albigard staggered upright and grabbed Len before he could crumple to the ground, an ironic reversal from mere moments ago.

The male Forsaken emerged from the tree, stepping over the bodies without sparing them a glance.

"Portal," the female Forsaken snapped, bracing the magical barrier in front of them with both hands, as more attacks from the guards burst against it.

The male Fae whistled sharply. In his peripheral vision, Len saw him make a curt gesture with one hand. A moment later, a portal flamed into existence, and he stepped through it. Albigard dragged Len through after him, the pair of them collapsing onto the vine-choked ground as soon as they reached the other side. The woman followed a moment later, still with her hands raised to hold the shield in place on the other side of the tunnel in reality. She let her arms fall to her sides as the portal snapped shut.

Len lay in a tangle with Albigard and tried to breathe past the heavy block of ice crushing his chest. The seconds ticked by, and more portals opened in the overgrown clearing where they'd ended up. Wild Fae came through in ones and twos, some of them supporting injured comrades.

"That's everyone," said the male Fae who'd freed Albigard and presumably blown the head off a guard.

"No sign of pursuit?" asked the female Fae who'd held the shield for them. "Good, let's get back to camp and figure out our next steps."

She cast another portal, and strong hands pulled Len and Albigard to their feet. After another moment of dizzying dislocation, Len found himself in a rocky landscape overgrown with the ever-present massive flowering vines. The place seemed to be a narrow canyon between two cliff walls, with a fast-moving river tumbling along the middle. The shadowed entrances of caves half-hidden by vegetation loomed on either side.

And there were people here. Dozens of them, including children—all with the same ragged and unkempt look as their rescuers. Or were they kidnappers?

At this point, Len was almost beyond caring.

Thankfully, he was also starting to feel slightly less like he'd just inhaled an iceberg... though there was a definite buzz of energy surrounding him that was both similar to, and different from, the presence of his old, familiar specters.

This is your brain on dead Fae animus, a little voice in the back of his skull offered helpfully. He shook his head to dislodge it.

Next to him, Albigard wasn't faring quite so well. He looked as though his burst of activity during the brief battle had drained whatever paltry reserves of strength he'd had left, and the Fae holding him by the arm might be the only thing keeping him upright. Len moved to take his other arm, somewhat reassured by the fact that the Forsaken who'd pulled him to his feet and dragged him through the portal let him go without a fuss.

"We have injured," called the moss-haired woman, who seemed to be one of the leaders.

Most of the activity in the camp had ceased upon their arrival, as all eyes focused on them — but at that prompting, several people hurried forward to assist with the wounded Forsaken being supported by their comrades. When all of them had been led off toward the entrance to a cave, the man and woman who'd taken the lead during the battle turned to regard Albigard intently.

"Are we your prisoners?" Albigard asked without preamble, his exhaustion clear in his voice.

Len held his breath as he awaited the answer, since it was blatantly obvious that they were both outnumbered and outclassed by the group around them. If the Forsaken wished them ill, they were pretty much screwed.

"That rather depends," said the woman. Her tone was pensive as she paced a circle around them, studying them with a direct green gaze.

"On what?" Len pressed, when she didn't elaborate.

"On whether your companion is willing to assist in rescuing Dhuinne from its imminent dissolution and destruction," she clarified.

Len's gaze flew to Albigard, as the sense of the words penetrated.

"You're aware of the Wild Hunt's forays into the other realms, then," Albigard said, sounding almost relieved. "And the state of the veil separating Dhuinne from the human world?"

"Of course we are," snapped one of the male Forsaken who'd been supporting an injured comrade earlier. "Do you think we risked our lives to free you on a whim, *Unseelie*?"

"That's enough, Ruvik," said the woman, before returning her attention to Albigard. "As my clansmen says, we are indeed aware of the damage. Probably in more detail than you are. However, that does not answer my question."

Albigard's shoulders sagged. "The Hunt is tracking me across realms. I am already resigned to my own death" — Len's fingers tightened around his arm involuntarily — "but I have lacked any strategy that would give that death meaning, by stopping the damage being done to Dhuinne and the other realms."

The woman exchanged a long glance with her male counterpart, and nodded. "A good answer. In which case, you are our guests rather than our prisoners."

Len briefly considered feeling offended by the fact that his human opinion hadn't been consulted. Fortunately or unfortunately, he didn't have the energy to spare for offense right now.

"Great," he said, and gestured at Albigard's shackles. "In that case, can we please get this iron off him?"

The male Fae gave the heavy chains an uncertain look. "We have a few blacksmithing tools…"

Len sighed. "If someone can find a dagger with a narrow tip and a thin piece of metal like a pin or a length of wire, I'll pick the locks. *Again*."

At least this time, no one would be blasting deadly magic at him while he worked, and Albigard was probably too wiped out right now to accidentally poke Len in the hip with his dick.

"Doubtless you never foresaw this degree of demand for your lock-picking talent," Albigard murmured, though he still sounded utterly exhausted.

"Nope," Len agreed, deadpan. "It's safe to say I did not, in fact, foresee *any* of this."

THREE

Someone had already relieved Albigard of the dagger he'd taken from the female Fae during the fight, but within moments, a teenage girl in a shapeless thigh-length tunic approached and handed Len a small knife with a slender blade, along with a twisted bit of wire. Again, he was aware that he should probably be insulted by these people's complete dismissal of him as a threat, even while armed. But... they could also blast his head off with magic if he tried to threaten them, so fair enough.

"Go on. Sit down before you fall down," Len said under his breath, nudging Albigard toward a conveniently flat rock that was only partly covered by vines.

Albigard sat without comment—more proof, if any were needed, that he was running on fumes at this point in the proceedings. Len wanted to ask him about the dead guards. Specifically, he wanted to ask why their animus had hit him upside the head like a pair of frozen two-by-fours. The most he'd ever felt before when someone died in his presence was a wispy breath of chill brushing his skin. He restrained himself, though, cognizant of the watchful audience of Forsaken surrounding them.

"Hold still," he said instead, and set to work on the iron padlock securing the collar around Albigard's neck.

It took twenty minutes or so to get all three of the locks picked, probably because Len's hands were shaking the whole time. Eventually, though, he removed the final shackle from Albigard's left wrist and tossed the chains aside. He'd expected some expression of relief as the iron fell away, but the Fae just continued to sit motionless on the rock, staring at nothing.

The male Forsaken leader had been keeping a casual eye on Len's progress, but now that the job was done, he frowned. "Nezri," he called in a foreboding tone, and the female leader turned to look at him.

Then her attention moved to Albigard, and she frowned, too. "Oh. I see. That's... certainly a complication."

With an unpleasant jolt, Len realized that in the absence of the iron shackles, the other Fae could now sense Albigard's lack of magic. The last hope he'd been holding out that Albigard had somehow been mistaken about what had happened to him drained away.

Len rose cautiously, not sure what he thought he'd be able to do if the Forsaken suddenly turned on them, but feeling like he at least needed to be on his feet for whatever came next.

"He sacrificed his magic to protect me," Len said, trying to put force behind the words as he met the woman's eyes. "You were there, in the Courtroom. He was trying to keep me safe."

For the first time, the moss-haired Fae seemed to look at him properly, rather than dismissing him as unimportant. Len imagined he could see calculations running behind her cool gaze. Then she turned her attention to Albigard again.

"Well, Mab's *tits*. How are you even functioning right now, Unseelie?" she asked, only to shake her head briskly. "Ah, never mind. As I said before, this complicates matters… but perhaps it doesn't affect the ultimate goal so very much."

In other words, the Hunt can still eat Albigard whether he has magic or not, Len translated in the privacy of his thoughts. *Lovely.*

"Bring him inside," said the male leader, addressing Len directly. "He's not the first to show up here with his magic ripped out by the roots. We can at least help him rest easier."

Len wavered for a moment, but the truth was, if Albigard stayed where he was for much longer, he was going to end up passing out where he sat and tumbling straight off the rock he was perched on. There was some reassurance to be found in the fact that their rescuers didn't seem to be openly judgmental about Albigard's situation—and also that they'd apparently had some previous experience in dealing with it.

He slung Albigard's arm across his shoulder and levered the Fae to his feet, only to hesitate. "Hang on. What if the Hunt shows up while we're inside your cave?" he asked, suddenly unsure if this motley group had properly thought this plan through. "Your people could be in danger."

"We can't control what the Wild Hunt decides to do," said the woman—*Nezri*. "Normally, it would not be a concern, as it only attacks those it's been sent to execute. Whether that will still be the case is anyone's guess, now that it's had a taste of fresh blood in the other realms. Regardless, the sooner your companion recovers his strength, the sooner we'll be in a position to act."

Act how? Len wanted to ask. Albigard slumped against his side, and he swallowed the question in favor of tackling one step at a time. "If you say so. I think he's about to pass out on us, by the way; where do you want him?"

Nezri turned to the male leader. "Danon, find him a sleeping place in the cave and do what you can for him. Afterward, we need to have a meeting."

Danon nodded. "Agreed."

He gestured for Len to follow and led the way into one of the caves. Albigard's feet dragged, but he went where Len steered him. The natural cavern was much larger inside than Len would have guessed. It was lit by the flickering glow of several campfires bounded by stone rings and spaced evenly around the area. The inescapable, out-of-control plant life had crept past the edges of the cave mouth to gain a foothold inside, though the vines showed definite evidence of having been recently hacked away.

Danon led them to a low pallet near the back. There were other, similar pallets scattered around the cave—a few of them now occupied by Forsaken that Len recognized as having been among the injured from the earlier rescue operation. Poorly buried instincts made him itch to check on them and make sure they were getting competent medical care for their wounds in these primitive surroundings. Realistically, though, since they were Fae, Len gathered they'd heal up just fine without any help from him.

More importantly, he was needed elsewhere.

He helped Albigard onto the low pallet. The Fae curled onto his side in a fetal position, still in obvious agony after having his magic ripped from him.

"Stand away," Danon said, after giving Len an odd, sidelong look.

Len stepped back with reluctance, folding his arms to keep from fidgeting as the other man bent over Albigard, repeating the same odd procedure he'd done inside the tree cell before breaking Albigard's bonds. His hands hovered above the Fae's hunched body, sweeping over him in slow arcs without touching.

The arcane process took considerably longer this time, but eventually Danon placed one hand over Albigard's forehead and the other over his heart. Albigard arched and cried out, writhing as though trying to escape the contact. Len started to lunge forward, only to be brought up short by a slender hand holding him back with effortless, inhuman strength.

"Wait," Nezri said.

Len gritted his teeth, every muscle tense as Albigard made a bereft noise and went abruptly limp.

Danon straightened away, and Len jerked his arm out of Nezri's grip.

She let him go without comment.

"What did you do?" he demanded, crouching next to the pallet and stroking Albigard's hair out of the way so he could get two fingers on his pulse point.

"Cauterized the damage," Danon said tersely.

The words had a finality to them that sent a shiver down Len's spine. This wasn't a temporary magical injury that could be undone with a spell, or with true love's kiss like some kind of childhood fairy tale. Albigard's magic had been ripped away, and now the bleeding stump had been... *cauterized.* The Fae's heart beat fast, but strong and steady beneath Len's touch. It slowed to a more normal resting rate by gradual degrees, and Len eventually took his fingers away.

As he contemplated the reality of exactly what Albigard had done in an attempt to protect him, the chest-squeezing, out of control feeling that heralded an oncoming panic attack began to narrow his vision to a gray tunnel. He swallowed hard.

"I... um... I'm sorry, but I need one of you to influence me to be calm," he managed. "Preferably without any other deals or agreements attached."

He looked up, Nezri's green eyes catching and holding his as his vision wavered. She looked faintly confused, but something in his expression must have convinced her that doing what he'd asked would be simpler than dealing with an irrational human having a meltdown in the middle of her camp.

Her expression narrowed, her gaze pinning Len in place. "Be calm, human," she said, her Fae will swallowing his until the band of panic snapped, replaced by abrupt serenity.

She was strong. Stronger than Albigard, even. But the chilly cloak of fresh death draped over Len was also strong—more so than the animus of Yussef and Rosa and all his other human ghosts had ever been. He shook his head briskly, breaking free of her influence while maintaining his grasp on the calm she'd offered him.

"Thanks," he whispered, swallowing hard and licking his lips to moisten them—his tongue catching on the familiar metal ring piercing his lower lip.

Both of the Fae were looking at him intently now, brows furrowed. The similarity in their features struck him, making him wonder if they were siblings, or—

Twins.

The realization struck him all at once. Powerful twins in their prime... who'd fled into the wildlands, rather than be used as weapons of mass destruction in a never-ending cold war. Len blinked a couple of times and set aside that particular eureka moment, figuring that blurting it out might not be the most diplomatic idea right now. That assumed he was even right about it in the first place.

He looked down at Albigard instead. The Fae appeared to be deeply asleep, or possibly unconscious. Without attempting to wake him, it was difficult to tell which.

"Will he be all right?" Len asked.

"No," Nezri said bluntly. "But he will be better able to function after a few hours of rest."

Len cursed himself silently for an idiot. Of course Albigard wasn't going to be *all right*.

"I understand," he rasped.

"You seem very protective of him," Nezri observed neutrally.

Len glanced up at the pair of Fae flanking the pallet, but did not rise. "Well... he doesn't really have anyone else left, at this point." He drew a deep breath and plowed forward. "Look—I need to give you some information. It may be important for you to know. But before I do, I need your word that as long as we both agree to help against the Hunt, you won't harm either of us because of what I'm about to tell you."

Albigard stirred in his slumber, a wordless, unhappy murmur slipping past his lips.

The two Forsaken shared another of those speaking looks, communicating without words.

"As long as you agree to help us, and do nothing to hurt anyone in the camp, no one here will harm you," Nezri said carefully.

"As long as we do nothing to *physically* hurt anyone in the camp," Len insisted, painfully aware of the dangers inherent in bargaining with Fae. "Not hurt feelings or causing offense."

Nezri raised a slanted eyebrow at him. "Agreed. You have our word as leaders, on behalf of everyone here."

"Okay." Len swallowed again. "First off, Albigard is my... friend. We're close, even though he's Fae and I'm human."

Rans' ghost whispered across his memory. *That word you keep using... I don't think it means what you think it means...*

"How very odd," Nezri said.

"Is it going to be an issue?" Len pressed.

Danon frowned. "Why would it be?"

Some of the tension eased from Len's shoulders. "A number of Unseelie seem to think it's additional cause for contempt," he said. "That's all."

Nezri shrugged. "A number of Unseelie are piss-addled idiots. Go on... I gather there's more."

"Yeah. There is." Len steeled himself, still uncomfortable with saying the next part aloud. "This next part's actually the big one. You already know I have some ability to control the Hunt, or at least repel it, right? Well, that's because I'm a—"

Albigard inhaled sharply, his eyes flying open. His hand darted out to grasp Len's wrist, the grip tight enough to be painful. "*Don't,*" he hissed.

"—necromancer," Len finished.

FOUR

"Yes," Nezri said, still giving Len a rather odd look. "We'd noticed. It is rather difficult to miss. You reek—"

"Of death," Len finished for her. He sighed. "Right. Silly me."

"For what it's worth," Danon told him, "I didn't notice the stench until after we came through the portal to the staging location. But, yes, in here it's very… pronounced."

"You get used to it," Albigard said weakly, his grip sliding away from Len's wrist.

"I'll admit I hadn't considered the idea of using necromancy against an archetype of Dhuinne's destructive power," Nezri mused, obviously more intrigued than outraged.

"Believe me," Len said, "I was as surprised as you are when it attacked me but didn't kill me."

Danon snorted. "A good deal more so, I would imagine. It makes a kind of sense, though…"

Albigard was struggling to hold onto wakefulness, but he rallied long enough to say, "You'll hold to your word… you will not harm him?"

Nezri gave him a severe look. "We're not the ones who sacrificed magic for a lie, Albigard of the Unseelie," she retorted sharply.

Len winced as smoke rose from the verbal scorch marks.

"It's fine," he said, placing a hand on Albigard's shoulder. "They don't care, beyond the fact that it might turn out to be useful. Go back to sleep."

"Not yet," the Fae insisted. His hazy eyes moved between the twins. "You mentioned a meeting."

"Yes." Nezri eyed him, assessing. "We will convene here, since I doubt your ability to stand up at the moment, much less walk. I will gather the camp."

Len made a quick calculation. "The water in the river. Is it safe to drink?"

"Of course it is," Danon replied. "But there is water here." He gestured at a gourd sitting next to the fire, similar to the one that had been left for them in the tree cell.

Len gave him a strained smile. "Save it for someone who needs it more," he said, and was rewarded with a covert nod of approval from Albigard.

After the better part of a full day without food or water, Len was starting to feel the effects. However, he also had no idea if he was once more vulnerable to becoming a Fae's vassal, now that Albigard no longer had the magic to maintain their existing connection. As long as he could manage it, he figured it was safer to avoid finding out the answer to that question.

He gave Albigard's shoulder a quick squeeze of reassurance and rose, exiting the cave. Again, he was struck by the multigenerational nature of this small group of outcasts. Outside, children crouched by the riverbank, scrubbing clothes in the fast-moving water. Farther away, two women were busy butchering some kind of deer-like animal hanging by its back legs from a tree branch, their heads bent together in intimate conversation as they worked. They appeared middle-aged, maybe pushing the half-century mark if they'd been human. They weren't human, though... and for all Len knew, they might have been around to witness the rise and fall of Ancient Greece.

Curious gazes fell on him as he walked to the edge of the river, some way upstream from the kids washing clothes. He knelt on the uncomfortable pebbles forming the bank and drank from cupped hands, just as he had in the pocket realm. Then he fished out one of the energy bars Vonnie had given him and ate it, stuffing the foil wrapper back in his pocket when he was done.

He had a feeling that littering wouldn't go over too well in this place.

After washing his sad excuse for a meal down with more of the sweet river water, Len hurried back to the cave. He must've missed some kind of subtle signal in the camp, because the rest of the Forsaken were finishing up their tasks or putting them aside, and heading for the cave as well.

As he entered, he noted with a shiver of disquiet that the vines snaking around the edges of the cave's mouth had made noticeable progress since they'd first arrived, barely half an hour ago. He kept a nervous eye on the creeping greenery as he skirted it and returned to Albigard's side. Once there, he gave the Fae a critical onceover in the firelight.

He was still awake.

He still looked like shit.

But, in defense of whatever procedure Danon had used on him to cauterize the bleeding stump of his magic, he at least didn't look like he was in unbearable physical pain anymore.

"You want an energy bar?" Len asked quietly. "I've got one left."

"Save it for your own use," Albigard told him. "I will take advantage of our hosts' hospitality... when I can stomach the thought of food."

Len took that to mean Albigard was in no danger of becoming another Fae's vassal if he accepted a gift, even with his powers gone. Or... possibly he *was*, but it didn't matter because he expected the Hunt to get to him before it became an issue.

"All right," Len said, and settled into a cross-legged position next to the pallet. His hips and knees creaked in protest. It struck him that he'd spent more time sitting on the ground during the past week than during the previous five years combined.

Meanwhile, the other Forsaken had filed in and found places around the fire. Even the children were present, watching Len and Albigard with wide eyes. Once they were all settled, Nezri rose and cleared her throat, drawing everyone's attention.

"This human and this Unseelie have agreed to help us in our attempts to heal Dhuinne," she said in a loud, clear voice. "We will extend them our hospitality and protection in the meantime."

A general murmur went through the small crowd. It sounded agreeable enough to Len's ear, and he relaxed a bit.

Nezri's gaze fell on Albigard. "We have maintained spies in the city for some time. The Court is not unaware of the nature of the threat to our world, but they have chosen to do nothing in response to the oncoming catastrophe. Nothing *constructive*, at least."

Arms crossed over his chest, Danon was leaning against a jutting stalagmite. Or stalactite? Whichever one grew out of the floor, anyway. Len could never remember.

"That leaves us to deal with it," he said. "The Forsaken have more of a connection with Mother Dhuinne than the Seelie or Unseelie ever had. We can see what's happening to our realm."

"See it, yes," Albigard said weakly. "But do you have a plan to *fix* it?"

"We do," Nezri replied. "We intend to draw the Hunt to Chaima."

Albigard blinked. His mouth opened as though to say something, but no words came out.

When no one expanded on the statement, Len figured he might as well ask. So he did, raising a finger like someone requesting the floor in a business meeting. "Excuse me. Clueless human here. Who or what is Chaima?"

"The world tree," Albigard said, regaining the power of speech. "A metaphor describing Dhuinne's system of magic."

"*Metaphor*?" Nezri's eyes narrowed in disdain. "Unseelie fool. Chaima is no story told to children to help them sleep at night. It is the beating heart of our realm."

Seated on his borrowed cot with his arms wrapped around his knees, Albigard still looked like a stiff breeze would blow him over. He didn't back down, though.

"Indeed? Then pray tell me where in the realm this *beating heart* might be found. Dhuinne is not so vast that it hasn't been thoroughly mapped. Yet I cannot recall any maps showing a massive tree at the center. At least, none that don't also have 'Here Be Dragons' inscribed around the edges."

Len wasn't sure whether the return of Albigard's waspishness was something to feel relieved about or not. Judging by Nezri's expression, it was a good thing he'd extracted that promise about not hurting them just because they offended someone in the camp. She wasn't the only one looking scandalized, either.

It was Danon who took up the defense. "The world tree exists," he said. "It's protected, though. Only the sidhe can penetrate Dhuinne's magic and approach it directly."

That was enough to shut Albigard up, so Len gathered there must be something to Danon's words. He remembered all the times the cat-sidhe had brushed aside protective spells that were supposed to make something invisible.

I told you, youngling — your wards are nothing to me.

"Okay," Len said slowly. "So we lure the Wild Hunt to this tree somehow. Then what happens, exactly?"

Nezri's sharp gaze fell on him. "The branches and leaves of Chaima represent Dhuinne's life magic—the magic of the Seelie. The trunk represents neutral magic—the magic of the sidhe. The roots are elemental magic. Destructive magic, breaking down soil and water to feed everything above. Unseelie magic."

Len set aside the rational part of his mind that wanted to pick holes in the concept, since he was sitting in a cave in an alternate dimension, surrounded by *literal faeries*. Instead, he went with it, talking out the concept even as he let it sink into his brain.

"So... right now the leaves and branches are growing out of control, while the roots are sick?" he hazarded. "Too much life magic, not enough elemental magic?"

Nezri gave him an approving nod. "Exactly. Congratulations, human. You have grasped a concept that seems to be utterly beyond the mental capacity of Dhuinne's rulers."

Something about the idea tickled the edges of Len's awareness, but when he tried to focus on it, it slipped away.

"Again, though," he said. "If you lure the Hunt to this magic tree, how does that help?"

A white-haired woman with deep wrinkles carving her face spoke up. "The Wild Hunt and Chaima's roots are both forces of destructive magic. If the Hunt can be drawn into the caverns below the tree, it's possible it will become trapped by the roots and be reabsorbed into Dhuinne's heart, rebalancing what has become unbalanced."

Len tried to wrap his brain around that. "You think the tree will suck up the Hunt's destructive power like fertilizer, and send it up to the leaves and branches to even out the life magic that's been growing out of control?"

"Something like that," Nezri said, like a teacher congratulating a young child who'd very nearly succeeded in grasping an advanced concept.

Len looked to Albigard. "Could that work?"

Albigard opened his mouth... and closed it again. A look of faint bewilderment slid across his pale, finely sculpted features.

"If... one accepts the underlying premise of the world tree's physical existence, it is not outside the bounds of possibility," he said after a long pause.

Again, something niggled at the back of Len's mind. "Can I ask—did this imbalance in Dhuinne start before or after the Hunt went feral?"

He was fairly sure he already knew the answer, but Danon confirmed it. "Before. But if the Hunt is growing larger and stronger, its darkness may be enough to balance things out, once it's been absorbed by Chaima."

Again, Len had the sense of something important hovering just out of his mental reach. He refocused on the here and now, figuring it would come to him eventually... if it was going to come to him at all.

"Right," he said. "And you're hoping to convince the Hunt to come to this underground cavern by using Albigard—"

"As bait. Yes," Nezri finished for him, not sugar-coating it. "And as he has already acknowledged, it is very likely that he will die during the attempt."

If people kept randomly dumping Albigard's approaching death at Len's feet enough times, would the idea eventually stop making his stomach twist and cramp?

For his part, Albigard seemed utterly fatalistic when it came to the danger. "Very well. In the absence of proof, I remain skeptical of the existence of Chaima as a real place. However, if one makes that logical leap, the underlying theory has some merit. In which case, the question becomes one of finding a sidhe to act as a guide for us. The cu-sidhe—"

"Won't help," Danon said with finality. "They've spent too long as the Court's lapdogs."

"We need the cat-sidhe," Len said, thinking of the diminutive Fae who'd helped them so many times already.

"Yes," Nezri agreed. "There is, however, a problem."

When isn't there? Len thought.

"What problem is that?" he asked, resigned.

Nezri's lips twisted in anger. "The cat-sidhe has been captured," she said. "They are being held prisoner in a secret location, by Oren of the Unseelie and those loyal to him."

Albigard eyes slid closed, his chin dipping to his chest as the words hit home.

FIVE

L en groaned. "Please tell me you're joking."

Nezri stared at him. "It is hardly a joking matter. Respect for the sidhe is another aspect of the delicate balance of Dhuinne. In past times, the Court would never have dared to lay hands on a sidhe."

"My father no longer counts his primary allegiance to the Court," Albigard said. "Nor to Dhuinne."

"Not even the Unseelie Court?" Danon asked, still propping up the jutting rock with his hip.

But Albigard shook his head. "I think not. He has allies, as you say, but he no longer speaks for the Unseelie. He was complicit in the recent attempt to abandon this realm and move the Fae Court to Earth. Indeed, it would not surprise me if he were the plan's mastermind."

Nezri crossed her arms, mirroring Danon. "That is a serious accusation."

"It is a serious matter," Albigard retorted.

She tilted her chin, acknowledging the words. "Whatever the case, we must stage a rescue before the Court has a chance to regroup... and before the Hunt tracks you here."

"Do you know where the cat-sidhe is being held?" Len asked, since that seemed like kind of an important question.

"No, but we don't need to," Danon said. "You've had contact with the sidhe recently. Their etheric fingerprints are all over that one." He gestured at Albigard.

"They offered their power to bolster my own so I could escape capture on Earth," Albigard said, sounding faintly ill. "No doubt that act of generosity was the only reason the guards were able to capture them."

"Probably," Danon agreed. "At any rate, with enough magical power, Nez and I can follow that trail straight to them."

"You are twins," Albigard said, not making it a question.

"Yes," Nezri confirmed. "We were acquainted with your sister and brother when we were younger. In the end, we had no desire to follow in their footsteps... so we left."

"You were wise to do so." The words were a whisper.

Albigard's siblings had been two more victims in the seemingly endless sea of casualties caused by the war between the Fae and the Demons. Worse, they'd been used as weapons, their formidable abilities burned out to commit genocide against an entire race. Len put a hand on Albigard's arm as a gesture of support, or... something.

"The practical upshot is this," Danon said. "When we act together, Nez and I can channel neutral magic, as well as elemental and life magic.

Now that we have a way to track the cat-sidhe, it won't matter what wards Oren and his cronies have placed around them. We can portal in, grab them, and portal out before the guards can mount much of a defense."

"How will you source the raw power to trace their location?" Albigard asked.

"We will have to draw from the other members of the camp," Nezri replied. "Those who agree to it, obviously."

Again, voices murmured around the fire.

Albigard's bloodshot gaze scraped over the ragtag group, assessing. "That may power your travel through wards to the cat-sidhe's location, but not with much to spare for any battle that might ensue afterward."

Danon started to reply, only to hesitate. Len took that to mean Albigard was right. He wavered for a moment, trying to think through possible scenarios, and spoke up before he could lose his nerve.

"I absorbed the, uh... the *animus* of the two guards who died when you got us out of the Dead Forest," he said. "It's not pleasant, but in an emergency Albigard was able to use power from my necromancy to fuel a portal between realms. He was sick afterward, though."

Albigard inhaled sharply, and Len turned to him, still gripping his arm.

"Don't get me wrong," Len told him. "I'm not happy about leaving you here alone, with no defense against the Hunt if it shows up. But... this sounds like an in-and-out operation. Smash and grab, and come right back here afterward, yeah?"

Albigard's eyes bored into him. "And will you accept a gift from one of them? Become their vassal so they may draw from you?"

Len quailed internally at the idea, but shoved aside his discomfort. "You're assuming I'm going to be alive long enough that I'll have a chance to regret it. If it's the price of getting one step closer to stopping the Hunt, do you really want me to say no?"

He was peripherally aware of the camp watching the exchange with interest. Meanwhile, Albigard looked like a man trying to come up with a rational argument and failing. Nezri spoke before he could formulate a response.

"That may not be necessary, human," she said. "We would have to test it—but if we combine our powers into neutral magic and you give us permission to draw from you, we may not need a gift or a bond."

Len remembered the battle in St. Louis... how the cat-sidhe had been able to draw from the Unseelie envoys. "So you could draw from me like a sidhe does, with no strings attached?"

Danon's brow furrowed. "Strings?"

"With no permanent bond in place," Albigard clarified.

"Perhaps," Nezri said.

Len released his hold on Albigard's arm and climbed to his feet. "Can we try it?"

"A small amount only," Albigard insisted.

"Are you worried about me, or about them?" Len asked.

"Yes," Albigard replied.

Which... *okay*.

Len cleared his throat. "Um, I should probably clarify that when I said it made Albigard sick when he used it, we're talking about 'vomiting up gouts of black bile and then nearly passing out' levels of sick."

Albigard shot him a look. "*Thank you*," he said peevishly.

Len shrugged. "It's the truth."

"We will test... *cautiously*," Nezri allowed.

"Right." Len shook out his arms, not sure exactly what to expect. "I just need to give you permission to draw power from me?"

Nezri and Danon exchanged a look.

"Permission for the purpose of..." Albigard interjected pointedly, still looking less than pleased by the whole thing.

Abruptly, Len remembered that he was making a deal with Fae—even if they were, like, *hippy* Fae. "Er, that is... I give you permission to draw power from me for the purpose of this test... and... if the test works, for the purpose of finding the cat sidhe, retrieving them, and getting back here safely. After which, I rescind that permission and would require it to be renegotiated if it became necessary again in the future."

Jesus. It was like the most convoluted kink negotiation Len had ever conducted before a bondage scene, and then some.

"We agree to your restrictions," Nezri replied. "We will test the concept now."

He watched nervously as the twins locked eyes once more. This time, the feeling of power growing and expanding between them was palpable, like a sudden pressure change in the air. After several interminable seconds of this, Len felt the sensation of an invisible hand reaching into his chest and tugging.

It wasn't a hard wrench, not like the time Albigard had pulled power from him to escape the pocket realm. By contrast, this was barely enough pressure to make him sway forward on his feet before righting himself.

Nezri's face twisted in distaste, and the sense of something being pulled from him disappeared abruptly. Len's ears popped.

"Yes, that is intensely unpleasant," she said.

"You're not wrong," Danon agreed. "It's still power, though. Better to have it if we need it than to not have it and die."

Len worked his jaw from side to side, trying to equalize the pressure inside his skull.

"I guess since the guards are already dead, they might as well be useful," he managed, still deeply uncomfortable with the idea of using the deceased as batteries.

Albigard looked up at him. "I don't like this," he said, the straightforward declaration taking Len by surprise.

He inhaled, choosing his words carefully. "Well, like I said—I'm not too thrilled about leaving you here defenseless, either. But we can't move forward with the rest of the plan until we get the cat-sidhe back. If my going along with them increases the odds of success, I think we need to do it."

The Fae gave a small, resigned nod. "I won't argue the fact that it's the best path to success. I merely state that I do not like it."

The mushy, emotional feeling flooding Len's chest wasn't super-useful under the current circumstances, but even so, he couldn't seem to stem it. "We'll be quick. In and out, then right back here. Just try not to get your soul eaten before then, okay?"

"It would hardly help matters if I allowed myself to be consumed before you return with the sidhe," Albigard told him.

Len nodded. "Damn straight." He returned his attention to the twins. "So, are we going right away, or what?"

Danon gestured to a couple of the camp members, who rose and headed deeper into the cave.

"Waiting gains us nothing, and could cost us much if the Hunt is close," Nezri said.

The two Fae who'd left returned bearing weapons—swords and daggers in leather sheathes; a brutal looking axe. The twins took the weapons and fastened them to their belts.

"We will still need to draw from the camp to power a portal leading to the cat-sidhe," Nezri told the assembled crowd. "If we are forced to use the necromancer's energy, it seems likely the effects will become debilitating shortly afterward. We'll hold his power in reserve to aid in our escape, should it become necessary."

Danon raised an eyebrow at Len. "Yes—quite so. Vomiting black bile, you said?"

"Seriously," Len confirmed. "It was like some next-level *Exorcist* shit. Zero out of ten, would not recommend to others."

Albigard shot him another unamused look.

"Enough talking. Let us depart," Nezri said, double-checking her weapons. "Danon will lead the way. Necromancer, you will come through last. Stay behind me, and as soon as we free the cat-sidhe and open an escape portal, use it. We will follow."

Albigard's expression remained stoic, but pale. He had the air of someone who really wanted to raise an objection, but was restraining himself from doing so.

"Hey. Don't worry, all right? We'll be back before you know it," Len told him, and hoped he wasn't lying.

Danon addressed the camp again. "Everyone who's willing to do so, please make your power available to us now." His eyes flicked to Len. "Guess I don't really have to say this, but there's no way of knowing what's likely to be on the other end of this portal."

"As long as the cat-sidhe's there," Len said. "That's all that matters."

The Forsaken warrior nodded. He closed his eyes, and Nezri did the same. They turned toward an empty part of the cave, and the sense of power growing in the air pushed at Len's eardrums again—far stronger this time. He squared his shoulders, meeting Albigard's green eyes for a final quick glance as a swirling vortex formed in front of the twins. The center darkened, becoming murky.

Half-seen images flitted across the space, shifting and changing like blowing sand. A forest. A river. A field of grass. A massive ruin, like an ancient church left to fall into decay as it was absorbed back into nature.

The view narrowed, rushing toward the collapsed walls and tilted towers. Len had a stomach-swooping sense of the view plunging *down*, like cresting the top of a rollercoaster. Abruptly, the vortex went black as pitch.

"Be ready," Nezri said, and Len realized with a jolt that he *wasn't* ready... he wasn't ready for any of this, what the hell had he even been *thinking*—

The edges of the vortex burst into flame, becoming a portal. "*Now!*" Danon barked, and leapt through the burning oval. Nezri followed—hands raised, ready to cast magic in attack or defense.

Len sucked in a sharp breath and lunged after her, emerging into blackness so complete that the crackling orange glow of the portal didn't even make a dent in the murk. It snapped shut an instant after he was clear of it, and Len couldn't have seen his hand in front of his face if he'd used it to slap himself.

He didn't dare move, didn't dare call out, for fear of alerting guards or worse. The place stank of mildew and rot. Before he could properly begin to panic, one of the Fae twins cast a glowing ball of light. It rose above their heads, but even magical light struggled to cut through the heavy blanket of darkness. A second sparkling ball joined the first, adding enough illumination to properly see their surroundings — which appeared to be an ancient underground vault.

The walls were rough-cut stone, slimy with age and damp. The floor was dirt... or maybe it had once been stone as well, but it had long since been reclaimed by the creeping earth. Aside from sickly blooms of fungi clinging to the crumbling walls, the place was free of Dhuinne's rampaging plant life.

Maybe that wasn't surprising, since it lacked even the barest hint of light.

Nezri and Danon stood ready for anything that might come their way as they looked around the echoing space. Danon froze and caught his breath.

"There," he said, and started toward the far end of the vault, still cloaked in darkness to Len's human eyes.

The glowing orbs floated in that direction as well, spreading their pool of light until it slid over a raised plinth, like a pagan altar. The two Fae hurried forward, Len following a couple of steps behind, as he'd been told. When he got close enough to make sense of the dark lump of a shape lying on the plinth, he inhaled sharply, fear and anger slamming into him in a tangled mass.

A battered black cat lay unmoving on its side, one ear tattered and chunks of fur missing from its body. Around its neck, a thin iron collar circled bare, blistered skin — a chain running from the restraint to a heavy bolt driven into the stone.

SIX

L en twitched, barely able to stop himself from lunging toward the unmoving cat. He burned with the need to check for a pulse, for breathing — any sign of life.

Before he could decide whether to push past the twins and take his chances, a low growl rumbled around the stinking space, raising the hairs on the back of Len's neck. Red eyes glowed in the dim light as a darker shadow emerged from behind the plinth. The outline was vaguely familiar, and it made Len's right hand itch for a canister of pepper spray.

"*Cu-sidhe*," Nezri said, voice tight. She and Danon both dropped into fighting stances, leaving Len to wonder why the buggering *fuck* one of the dog-like sidhe was being used as a guard for the cat-sidhe. Shouldn't they be on the same side?

"Are we sure the cu-sidhe isn't a prisoner here, too?" Len asked, backing up a few steps so he wasn't crowding Nezri in case they needed to fight.

The hellhound sprang for Danon, who darted sideways with a cry and slashed at it with his sword.

"Okay, guess not," Len muttered, as his heart thundered in his throat.

Nezri flung a blast of crackling magic at the beast, but it seemed to slide off the hound's matte black hide without doing damage. Len inched backward until his shoulders met the slimy, mold-covered wall as the fight exploded into the open space in front of the stone altar. He eased sideways as the cu-sidhe and the Forsaken lunged and slashed in a deadly dance, until he was able to slip behind the plinth and get a closer look at the injured cat.

He let out a sigh of relief as he saw the animal's flank rising and falling in a rapid, shallow rhythm. *Alive.* That relief fled a moment later when he examined the iron collar and chain, looking for the padlock securing it.

There was no padlock.

The metal had been welded shut, leaving scorched hair and skin beneath the join. Cold rage bubbled in Len's stomach, competing with a jabbering refrain of *oh shit, oh shit, how do I get them loose*?

Danon cried out—a roar of pain and anger.

"Axe!" Nezri snapped, and a moment later Danon's axe flew through the air and clattered against the wall a few feet away from Len.

Len stared at it, and then stared at the iron chain bolted to the stone plinth. "Oh my god, are you kidding me?" he said… but he scrabbled for the heavy tool and darted back behind the altar for cover with the handle clutched firmly in both hands.

The head of the axe was chipped in one corner where it had impacted the wall—not exactly a ringing endorsement for its sturdiness. Most of the blade was still intact, however, and it wasn't like they'd brought along bolt cutters or an acetylene torch to cut the chain.

Len — who had never wielded an axe in his damned life — said, "*Fuck!*" and hoisted the thing over his head like some kind of gay, blue-haired lumberjack. Directing the blow as far away from the cat as possible in case his aim was really, really bad, he clenched his jaw and let fly. The impact reverberated through his arms and shoulders as the blade hit the chain sitting on its solid stone base, and the noise made his ears ring.

He ducked an instant later as a blast of magic came within a foot of his head, slamming into the wall behind him with a shower of sparks. When he straightened, the balance of the axe in his hands felt wrong. Len looked at it stupidly, only then noticing that another large chunk of the metal blade had shattered during the blow. Fortunately, a glance at the chain revealed that it hadn't fared any better, and now lay in two pieces on the plinth.

The cat was still unmoving, except for its rapid panting — this, despite the deafening sound of axe against chain only a couple of feet away from its head. Len tried not to be too worried by that, since there were several more immediate worries to deal with at the moment. He scooped up the tiny creature and ducked behind the sturdy stone altar again, cradling the cat-sidhe to his chest.

"Human!" Nezri cried. "*Brace!*"

That sounded deeply ominous, and in reality, there was no good way to brace for the sensation of icy death being yanked through his chest and dragged out of his ribcage. Len gasped, feeling like his lungs had frozen solid — frost crackling across tender bronchi and alveoli.

Something cold and powerful slammed through the vault. The cu-sidhe yipped in pain, and two seconds later a strong hand pulled Len unceremoniously to his feet. His arms tightened around the cat, desperate not to lose his grip on the small creature as his body fought for air. The vault had fallen into darkness again, the glowing orbs extinguished by the freezing blast of death magic. When an oval bound by icy blue flame hissed into existence in front of him, the sudden brightness of it hurt his eyes. He flinched, but the hand wrapped around his bicep tossed him through the portal without ceremony.

Len fell to his knees in the cave, surrounded by Forsaken who exclaimed in surprise and started toward him, alarmed by his appearance... or maybe alarmed by the injured cat's appearance. Head spinning, Len tried desperately to twist sideways as he toppled toward the floor, not wanting to crush the little sidhe's battered body.

Arms caught him before he could hit the ground, taking his weight and cradling him against a lithe form. He blinked up, clutching the warm bundle of fur to his chest. Familiar green eyes lit by worry and relief filled his vision.

"You did it," Albigard breathed, even as two more figures tumbled out of the blue-ringed portal, crashing to the ground nearby. The portal irised closed behind them, leaving the cave in silence except for Len's ragged breathing and the twins' groans of distress.

Nezri and Danon hadn't fared much better than Albigard when it came to processing dead animus. The only saving grace was that unlike Albigard, they hadn't already been suffering from starvation and hypothermia before attempting to use it.

Danon had also taken a vicious bite wound to the forearm during the fight with the cu-sidhe, and Nezri had a claw slash across one thigh. Meanwhile, Len was uninjured—other than bruised knees from hitting the ground after being shoved through the portal. The sense of his internal organs having been flash-frozen subsided after a few minutes, leaving him feeling wrung out, but not nearly as drained as he had been after they'd escaped from the pocket realm.

Unfortunately, the cat-sidhe was another matter entirely.

The same elderly, white-haired female Forsaken who'd explained about the world tree's magic leaned over the pitiful form with Len, as they gingerly examined the shape-shifting Fae. Len peeled back one eyelid with a careful touch, revealing the nictitating membrane drawn across the eye, which had rolled back until the white was showing.

The old woman, who had been feeling around for broken bones, straightened with a disgruntled noise. "That anyone would *dare* treat a sidhe in such a way," she muttered. "Chained in iron, no less! Leesa—go find me a file. There should be one among the blacksmithing tools."

The teenage girl who'd been hovering nearby nodded and hurried off.

Len ran a hand over his face. "If we can get the collar off, will their injuries heal? These burns, along with the lack of pupillary reaction—if this were an animal on Earth, I'd be really worried about hypovolemic shock right now. But unless you're hiding some advanced medical equipment in the back of the cave, I've got no way to push fluids."

"I don't know what that means, human," said the old woman. "But as long as the sidhe was not attacked magically as well as physically, they should recover with a few hours' rest. And once they do, I would not want to be the person who did this to them."

For the dozenth time since he'd first met a Fae, Len forcibly readjusted his worldview to '*this is fine; these horrific injuries just need a nice afternoon nap to heal.*' He should know better by now, he supposed—even if the reality went against a lifetime of earthbound medical knowledge.

Leesa returned with a rough metal file and started patiently sawing away at the collar under the white-haired woman's supervision. Len waited and watched until the iron circlet had been safely removed, and the cat arranged comfortably in a nest of blankets near one of the fires.

Albigard had returned to his borrowed pallet earlier, since he had little to offer the cat-sidhe in the absence of his magic. He looked up as Len approached. "How are they?"

"Burned," Len said, lowering himself to sit next to the Fae. "Battered. Unconscious. Not collared with iron anymore, at least. What about the twins?"

"Resting," Albigard told him.

He nodded. "You should take a page out of their book. We're not going anywhere until the cat-sidhe has recovered, and you still look like hell."

Albigard raised an eyebrow. "Do try not to be *deliberately* insulting."

It wasn't so much the observation that he looked terrible, Len knew, as the invocation of the demon realm that had offended him.

"For humans, it's only a saying," he reminded the Fae patiently. "Okay, fine. You still look like *shit*. Is that better?"

"Arguably," Albigard replied. "What about you? Are you well?"

Len tried to decide how to frame his answer. "I... guess so? Honestly, I'm not sure what measuring stick I'm supposed to use under these circumstances. I'm not badly drained, though. Not like last time. Apparently, the twins didn't even need all of the animus I got from the two dead guards to knock out the cu-sidhe and portal us back here."

Albigard tilted his head, considering. "Your previous... *specters*... were only human. Fae lives— or Fae deaths, in this case—contain far more raw power. It's a fundamental difference between the species."

Longer life spans. Amazing healing powers. Magic.
Len supposed it made sense that a dead Fae might
act as a heavy-duty industrial battery, compared to
a human acting as an Energizer double-A.

"Still not sure I'm on board with this necromancy thing," he grumbled. "Using the dead like
that..."

"Well," Albigard pointed out mildly, "you
were the one to suggest it, in this particular case."

"Yeah," Len agreed. "I'm painfully aware, believe me."

"And it worked," Albigard continued. "The
cat-sidhe is here. We are one step closer to containing the Hunt, if all this talk of Chaima is not pure
fantasy."

Len eyed him curiously. "Are you seriously
trying to give me a pep talk right now?"

"Merely stating fact," said the Fae.

"Huh." He took a slow breath and let it out,
trying to ease the tension in his shoulders. "Well...
like I said, you should get some rest. Unless the
Hunt shows up, nothing's going to happen for the
next few hours. And when we're ready to move,
you'll need all the energy you can get."

"And you? Will you rest as well?" Albigard
asked.

He probably should. Too bad he was so wired
after the cat-sidhe's rescue that he was practically
climbing the walls. "I don't think I can right now.
Too much leftover adrenaline still sloshing
around."

"Understandable."

Len scrubbed at his hair, which had long ago given up any pretense of being styled. "Assuming our hosts don't mind, I might walk around a bit. Talk to people. This place is kind of fascinating... and, uh, not at all what I'd pictured, after your description of the Forsaken."

Albigard shot him a wry look. "Fantasy and reality are often entirely different prospects. Perhaps we should count ourselves lucky that our new allies are not, in fact, sex traffickers and slavers."

"You know, I really can't argue with that sentiment," Len agreed. He hooked a hand around the back of Albigard's neck and rubbed his thumb over the smooth skin at the corner of his jaw, watching the Fae's eyes slide shut beneath the gentle touch. "Go on—sleep. I'll check in, and wake you up whenever something interesting happens."

SEVEN

After finding the white-haired female elder — whose name was apparently Aesulna — Len asked if he'd be bothering anyone by wandering around a bit and asking questions. She assured him that he had the run of the camp, and that anyone who didn't want to talk to him would simply tell him so.

It seemed unbelievable that it was barely mid-afternoon, given everything that had happened since he and Albigard had been hauled off to face the Fae Court that morning. While it was tempting to assume that time moved strangely in Dhuinne, Len knew that wasn't it. They just hadn't stopped for breath since then — or at least, Len hadn't.

He emerged from the cave, the entrance of which was now more than halfway concealed by vines. The most aggressive tendrils had encroached several yards into the cavern, twining along the walls and floor. Outside, things were just as bad. Worse, even. Paths that had been wide enough for two people when he'd come outside to get a drink from the river earlier, were now a tight squeeze for one.

Several of the camp members were occupied with hacking back the choking jungle of foliage — apparently a full-time job in and of itself. Len wondered if Dhuinne had seasons. Would cold weather freeze the out-of-control greenery into submission for part of the year? He made his way to the river's edge and drank some more of the clear, sweet water, then wavered for a few moments over the prospect of eating his last energy bar.

In the end, he decided to hold onto it for now. For one thing, he was still some way off from real hunger—the kind he'd experienced after days spent without food in the barren pocket realm. And for another, he suspected that, in a pinch, Albigard would be able to accept food from their hosts and give it directly to Len, as a way to get around the danger of him accidentally falling into another gift-bond with a Fae.

He splashed a bit of cold water on his face and went to talk with the camp members who were busy beating back the encroaching vines. Leesa was there, and happily handed him the rough iron hoe she'd been using to hack at the plants. From the others on the plant-control crew, he learned that Dhuinne did not, in fact, have seasons. Not beyond the rainy season and the dry season, anyway.

This, they informed him, was the dry season. Len could barely imagine what the job of keeping the paths clear would be like when it was raining every day.

One of the men asked a tentative question about his necromancy, and Len answered as best he could... which admittedly wasn't very well.

"Apparently, in a pinch I could even draw power from dead plants," he concluded, gesturing with the hoe at the vines they'd been battling.

"Though I don't get the impression any of these are in danger of actually dying."

Indeed, many of the dismembered plants were already sending out tentative new shoots into the pathway. As an experiment, they dug up one of the vines by the roots, and Leesa set it on fire with a gesture of one hand and an expression of deep concentration. Len closed his eyes, and thought he felt a hint of a cool, ineffable breeze caress his face.

"Did it work?" Leesa asked, bright-eyed and curious.

Len opened his eyes again. "I think so. I felt something, but it was faint. Still, I'd much rather get energy from dying plants than from dying animals or people."

The man who'd asked about Len's powers tilted his head, considering. "You a vegetarian, then?"

"Well... no," Len said.

The male Fae shrugged. "Then you're already getting energy from dying animals. And if you're going to hunt or butcher an animal anyway, isn't it best to use everything you can? 'S just wasteful otherwise, if you ask me."

Len blinked, not able to come up with a decent argument against that. At least, not beyond '*You're probably right, but it still creeps me the hell out.*'

"I... guess there's something to that, yeah," he acknowledged.

They finished clearing the path, and Leesa dragged Len away for a proper tour of the area of the river basin that the Forsaken had claimed as their own. She rattled off details about the way the protective wards were set up, obviously fascinated by magic and the theory behind it. Most of it meant very little to Len with his prosaic human background, but he could still appreciate her enthusiasm for the subject.

She showed him the smithy where they made their crude iron tools, and the cave where they stored preserved food. They stopped and chatted with other people along the way, most of whom were happy to take a break from their work for a few minutes.

Len wanted to ask them why they'd joined the Forsaken camp—whether they were criminals, or political dissenters, or conscientious objectors, or what. It seemed rude, though, so he didn't.

As they were heading up a steep trail toward what Leesa insisted was the highlight of the tour, she turned to look at him. "Your friend seems really sad," she said, out of the blue.

Len nearly tripped over a rock, taken by surprise at the observation. He cleared his throat. "Um, yeah—he's completely miserable. His father hates him, he's lost his magic, two of his closest friends are dead, and he's probably going to die trying to help capture the Wild Hunt. Honestly, I'm surprised he's coping as well as he is."

It was a lot to dump on a teenager, but she and the other children had been present during the strategy meeting right along with the rest of the group. Len got the impression that they didn't coddle their kids here.

She pondered that for a few moments, making her way slowly up the path.

"I think it's good that he's got you, so at least he's not all alone," she said eventually. And then, "Is it strange being a human?"

That startled a snort from him. "*Strange*? Why do you ask? Is it strange being a Fae?"

She shot him a sheepish smile. "Sorry, I guess that was a stupid question, huh?"

"Nah," Len said. "Not really. I'm kind of a strange human, to be honest—even back home. And being a human in Dhuinne is *definitely* weird."

Her smile broadened. "How do you get your hair that color? I've never seen blue before—only green and brown from plant dyes. It's pretty."

"It's just a different kind of dye," he told her. "You can get all sorts of different colors on Earth. 'Fraid I don't know what's in it, though."

At that, she gave him an exaggerated frown. "You put dye on your head without knowing what's in it?"

He chuckled in spite of himself. "Well, in my defense, someone else is supposed to test it first to make sure it's safe."

She weighed that.

"And I guess since you're here trying to lure the Wild Hunt into a trap, it's pretty far down the list of things that are likely to kill you?" she suggested.

"You've got that right," he said ruefully.

She smiled again, tentative this time. "Well... in case no one else has said it, thanks for doing what you're doing here." Her expression sobered. "Things in Dhuinne are getting really messed up.

It's been bad my whole life, but... it's been getting a lot worse recently. You know?"

It was Len's turn to be silent for a few steps. "I do. It's started affecting my world, too. And... I don't know for sure if my being here will make a difference at all. But since there's a chance, I have to try, right?"

She nodded. "Yes. I suppose so. But we still appreciate it."

Len's throat absolutely did *not* close up in response to the simple, guileless declaration. He swallowed a couple of times, and said, "Do me a favor? Tell Albigard that same thing when you get a chance. Only... don't be offended if he gets all prickly about it afterward."

She nodded. "I will." With a deep, cleansing breath, she indicated an aperture in the jutting cliff face. "Anyway, here we are. I think this place is why the camp actually decided to settle here originally. I'm not allowed, but you can go in."

Len gave her a curious look. "Why aren't you allowed?"

Her nose wrinkled up. "I'm too young." When that didn't clear Len's expression of confusion, she spelled it out for him with all the world-weary wisdom of a teenager. "The adults come here to have sex a lot. Nezri and Aesulna say maybe in a couple of years they'll let me in." Her eyes slid to the side.

"But?" Len prompted.

He watched her debate with herself for a moment before making a decision.

"But... I might have sneaked in a few times when no one else was there," she admitted, quickly adding, "We all do it—it's not just me. Anyway, you should go see. It's a hot spring—it comes right out of the heart of the mountain. If your friend's feeling better tonight, maybe you can bring him here. It'll help him relax."

Len blinked, his eyebrows climbing as he tried to decide if that was supposed to be innuendo or not. And... what the hell. Under the circumstances, he figured he might as well ask.

"Was that supposed to be innuendo?"

She shrugged one skinny shoulder. "Not really. It's nice just to soak, too." She looked at him speculatively—the expression of someone on the trail of hot gossip. "Why... are you and him lovers? Really?"

Visions of being hauled before the camp elders on charges of corrupting the youth floated through Len's head, but at least it was a chance to test the waters with someone who didn't seem overly offended by the topic.

"Would it be a problem if we were?"

This time, the shrug raised both of her shoulders. "It's just odd, thinking about a human and a Fae together, that's all. Not my business, though—forget I asked."

A human and a Fae. Not two men together.

"Well," he told her, "we've already established that I'm an odd human." He hooked a thumb toward the gap in the stone walls. "It sounds really nice; I'll go check it out. Thanks for giving me the tour—and for being the nicest Fae I've met to date."

She chuckled. "What... even nicer than your friend?"

"*Much*," Len said emphatically, drawing a real laugh from her.

Once she'd headed down the trail, skipping nimbly over the uneven rocks and ducking the jutting branches, Len turned to examine the irregular opening in the cliff face with interest. Humidity choked the air coming from inside. He peered in. The space beyond wasn't a cave, exactly. Light filtered down through gaps in the stone arches and columns that enclosed the rocky, steaming pools of cloudy water.

Less of an attempt had been made here to beat back the ever-present tropical vines, and the heavy scent of flowers perfumed the air. The topography of the rugged mountainside diverted the water from the hot spring into several pools of varying sizes—those higher up spilling over to fill those further down the slope. A handful of Fae lounged in the pools alone or in pairs—all naked, as far as Len could tell.

Some of them looked up as he passed through the entrance.

"Erm, hi. Am I intruding?" he asked cautiously.

Two of the women had been pressed together intimately when he entered, nuzzling each other's faces. They turned, and Len recognized the pair that had been butchering the deer earlier.

"Come in, as you like," said the one who'd been straddling her companion's lap in the water. "Or don't. It's nothing to us, human."

The words were brusque, but not delivered in anger. The speaker returned to her exploration of her companion's lips without waiting for an answer.

With that indifferent offer of permission extended, Len walked farther into the fantastical space, picking his way along a path that seemed to have been smoothed by Fae hands, with the rough rocks carved into steps leading to the higher pools. He looked around with something like awe, taking in the play of light and shadow through the steam… the green and blue and violet of the flowering vines.

It was, in a word, magical—the faerie realm, laid bare beneath the eyes of a human.

He made his way to a vantage point with a flat rock that hadn't been completely choked by plant life, and sat, taking it all in. Thick moss clung to the stone, cushioning it—the same blue-green as the stuff that had been growing on the floor of the Court building like a carpet. True to the female Fae's word, none of the others seemed to pay his presence here much mind.

Len stayed and listened to the burble and splash of water against stone, letting the serene surroundings leach some of his cares away, at least for a time. Other members of the camp came and went as the angle of the light filtering into the grotto tilted into deepening shadow. Some of the bathers chatted in low voices, and at one point the sound of female pleasure crested and ebbed.

He let it all wash over him, watching in wonder as little glowing lights flickered into existence one by one in the deepening dark—like fireflies hovering among the green leaves, but bright enough to illuminate the area as the sun went down. The pools themselves also seemed to emit a soft glow, as though lit from within.

Reluctantly, Len rose and picked his way down the path. Though he would have liked to stay longer, he was unwilling to risk the trail leading down the mountain in full darkness. It was also past time to check on things back at the cave.

He was most of the way down when a familiar figure jogged toward him. Leesa slowed when she recognized him. Her grin was a slash of white teeth in the deepening dusk.

"The cat-sidhe is awake! You should go back to the cave. There's going to be another meeting!" she exclaimed breathlessly, brushing past him to continue up the trail—presumably to inform the bathers of the same thing.

EIGHT

Len resisted the urge to hurry, not willing to risk a fall and a broken leg on the rocky path. When he finally reached the cave, it was to find most of the camp already assembled. He skirted the edges of the group, looking for Albigard.

It was a testament to how badly Albigard had needed rest that he was still sprawled on his pallet, fast asleep and oblivious to the murmurs of excitement building around him. Len crouched and placed a hand on the Fae's shoulder. For an instant, he flashed back to the moment in the pocket realm when Albigard had awakened explosively, hurling magic before he was even properly aware of his surroundings.

Hard on the heels of that came the realization that Albigard wouldn't be hurling magic at Len or anyone else... not ever again.

The Fae blinked awake, disoriented for a moment before his gaze sharpened. "The cat-sidhe?" he asked hoarsely.

"Conscious, apparently," Len told him. "The camp is gathering."

Albigard rolled into a sitting position, looking markedly stronger than he had earlier. Len rose, scanning the crowd by firelight until his eyes landed on a familiar pixie-like figure seated on a pile of blankets. The cat-sidhe—now in humanoid form—was deep in conversation with Aesulna, sipping steaming liquid from a cup.

Nezri approached Albigard's pallet. Her skin was still pale after her adventure with necromancy earlier, and the dark circles under her eyes looked like bruises. "You're both here. Good. We must discuss our plan with the cat-sidhe, now that they appear to be somewhat recovered." The female twin's voice betrayed nothing of whatever weakness still plagued her.

Danon, meanwhile, was making his way toward the sidhe—looking every bit as pasty-faced as his sister. Len met Albigard's eyes and extended a hand to him, hoisting the Fae to his feet when he accepted it. They followed Nezri toward the little group, where someone handed Albigard a cup of whatever steaming stuff the sidhe was drinking. He accepted it with a nod of thanks and sipped.

The cat-sidhe looked up as Len and Albigard arrived, a combination of relief and disquiet lighting their expressive eyes. "You're safe. Good."

Scabs and bruising darkened one side of the sidhe's face, and livid red marks ringed their neck. The cartilage of one delicately pointed ear was torn. The injuries appeared several days old, however—already half-healed. Len knew that in another day or two, no physical evidence of the abuse would remain.

Idly, he wondered if all of the guards who'd attacked the sidhe in California had survived the fight.

Albigard, too, seemed to be transfixed by the sidhe's injuries. He blinked, breaking free of his reverie. "I'm not certain *safe* is the right word. But the Forsaken have a theory, and I would very much like your opinion on it."

The cat-sidhe gave a nod of encouragement and took another sip of their drink.

"The people here believe that Chaima is a physical place—a real tree—and that if I can draw the Wild Hunt into the caverns that house its root system, Dhuinne may be able to absorb it and use the destructive magic to rebalance its rampaging life magic."

The cup froze an inch from the diminutive Fae's lips, and they blinked. Silence settled over the gathered crowd, as complete as though everyone in the camp was holding their collective breath, waiting for an answer.

The sidhe lowered the cup carefully and set it aside. "That... is not an approach I had considered. The Hunt is not the underlying cause of the magical imbalance in Dhuinne. It is only one symptom."

"Is Chaima real, though?" Albigard insisted.

"Yes, of course it is," the cat-sidhe replied. "That is the same as asking if Dhuinne is real. One is a reflection of the other."

"And you could take us there?" Albigard asked.

Again, the sidhe hesitated. "Not at this precise moment... but when I have recovered more fully, yes."

"Do you think it could work, though?" Len demanded, trying very hard not to focus on what it would truly mean if the sidhe said yes.

He could almost see the calculations running behind the sidhe's sharp, catlike eyes.

"I think... your proposed plan could quite possibly succeed in containing the Hunt and bringing it back under control," they said slowly. "I am less certain that it would repair the underlying damage to Dhuinne. However... the theory of rebalancing life magic with excess elemental magic seems sound. It might function as a temporary measure while the true cause is found and addressed."

Len swallowed, still refusing to think beyond the next step in the journey... the next link in the chain. "How long will you need to recover from your injuries? Because the Hunt could show up here at any time, and if it does, these people are in terrible danger."

"We will leave in the morning," the little sidhe declared. "The Hunt is not currently within the realm of Dhuinne. We have time."

Len's stomach dipped. "Does that mean it's on Earth?"

"That I do not know, human. I only know that it is not here." Green eyes met his. "I am sorry."

Albigard's cool fingers brushed Len's, and the Fae tangled their hands together, startling him. Len looked at the hand holding his, then up at his companion's face.

"Tomorrow," Albigard said softly. "We will fix this tomorrow."

Len struggled to get his plunging stomach and paralyzed lungs under control, trying not to imagine how much damage the Wild Hunt might do to Earth in the course of a single night.

"Tomorrow," he rasped in weak agreement.

"Shall we accompany you on your journey?" Danon asked, gesturing at his sister.

A small, sad smile lifted the corners of the sidhe's lips, only to fade away an instant later. "No, younglings. Your power is vast, but you cannot assist in this. Stay with your tribe and keep them safe. In fact, you should probably decamp from this place for a few days."

"Even with wards in place, my presence here has put you all at risk," Albigard said. "The Hunt will sense that I have been here, and may pass through the camp as it tracks me."

Nezri nodded. "To move elsewhere for a short time is no great hardship—especially if we are able to return afterward. It is a small price to pay for Mother Dhuinne's survival."

"Then we will all depart tomorrow at dawn," said the cat-sidhe. "Until then, rest and fortify yourselves. I intend to do the same."

"Your injuries," Len said, desperate to keep his focus anywhere but where it wanted to go—to Earth, and his friends there who might be in terrible danger. To what they would all have to face in the morning. He swallowed hard. "I have medical training. Is there anything I can do to make you more comfortable?"

The sidhe graced him with the same small smile they'd bestowed on the twins. "No, human. Someone else needs you far more than I, tonight."

And with that, Len and Albigard were effectively dismissed. The plan was in place, and nothing else remained to be discussed. Members of the camp began to disperse to their various campfires, discussing the day's events in excited tones.

Meanwhile, Len stood frozen, unable to move for fear that it would shatter the brittle shield he was holding around his emotions.

Leesa approached them nervously, casting Len a concerned look before turning her attention to Albigard. "I have a message from the members of the camp," she told him. "We want you to know how grateful we are for what you're doing. It's very brave, and we'll never forget it."

Albigard was, for one of very few times in Len's experience, struck speechless.

Leesa hurried on. "It's all right, you don't have to say anything. Just… thank you." With that, she darted in and kissed Albigard on the cheek, then turned and hurried away.

Albigard lifted a hand to the side of his face, then blinked, coming back to himself. "No wonder they live in exile in the wildlands," he said. "Such softness would not survive a week in the city."

Len wanted to grab the conversational life preserver—to chide Albigard for being an ungracious asshole to the bitter end. He didn't. He *couldn't*.

Albigard's brows drew together. "Are you well?"

"No," Len said hoarsely. "No, I'm really not. Will you… come with me? There's a place I want you to see."

Someone pushed a leaf-wrapped package of food into Albigard's hands as they made their way toward the entrance of the cave. Two Fae were hacking away at the vines that had, by this point in the evening, nearly blocked the opening in its entirety.

He and Albigard squeezed past the choking plant life. Len came to an abrupt halt outside, upon seeing that the entire canyon was now alight with little glowing spheres, each pulsing slowly in an irregular pattern.

"What are those things?" he asked. "The firefly things, I mean."

Albigard barely spared them a glance. "They're only sprites. A far more pleasant and useful nocturnal denizen than the night-scuttles, to be sure."

Len had been worried that he was going to have to hang onto Albigard's arm and use him as a seeing-eye Fae to get where they were going, but the scores of floating sprites illuminated their surroundings like strings of ever-shifting Christmas lights.

"They're amazing," he breathed, letting the vision of unearthly beauty chase his unwanted thoughts into the background, at least for a time.

"What is it you wanted to show me?" Albigard asked.

"It's a surprise," Len told him. "Come on— follow me."

He led the way to the switchback trail leading up the mountain, taking care with his footing— Albigard a steady presence at his back. After two trips up and one trip down, his thigh muscles were definitely feeling the burn. He hoped that wouldn't come back to bite him in the ass tomorrow, since he had no idea how much walking was likely to be involved with getting to the mythical world tree. At least the hot springs would help with his sore muscles.

It was worth every ache and twinge to see Albigard pause in the gap leading into the grotto with a soft exhalation. "*Oh.*"

In full darkness, the place was even more spectacular than it had been at dusk. The pools were very definitely glowing with their own pale, blue-gray phosphorescence, while the twinkling sprites threw a golden, shifting light across the curtains of vines and perfumed, trumpet-shaped flowers. The sound of water flowing over stone added a soothing background noise.

"If you're going to run away and live in the wilderness," Len offered, "this is certainly the place to do it."

"Indeed." Albigard sounded truly impressed, which was as much as Len could have hoped for.

Only a single Fae occupied the steamy space as they entered. Len recognized Danon lounging in one of the smaller middle pools, his arms spread along the rocky ledge at his back. He must have come straight here after the meeting broke up.

"Found this place already, did you?" he greeted.

"Leesa showed it to me while she was giving me the grand tour today," Len said. "She seems like a really good kid."

"She is," Danon agreed. "They're all good children. Sometimes I wish we could offer them more of a life than sleeping in caves and picking berries."

"I don't think she's complaining," Len told him. "I've seen the Court, and personally, I like this place a lot better."

"Seconded," Albigard murmured.

"Well, I hope you're right about that," Danon said. "Anyway, don't just stand there. Come on in. I just wanted a quick soak to loosen some of the knots. That power of yours is *not* my idea of fun, necromancer."

"Also seconded," Albigard deadpanned.

"Yeah… sorry about that," Len told them. "It's not something I asked for, believe me."

He led the way into the grotto and crouched next to the first pool, dipping a cautious hand in the water. It was hot, but not as hot as he'd thought it might be.

"Top pools are the hottest," Danon advised. "Bottom one is the coolest—though 'cool' is relative. You'll probably want one of the middle ones."

"Thanks," Len said, and headed to a larger pool just below the one the Fae was using.

Albigard followed at a slower pace, letting his fingers run over the moss-covered stones and the waxy leaves of the draping vines. Len realized he was staring at his companion, but there was something deeply satisfying about watching the tension drain from Albigard's shoulders as he closed his eyes, breathing in the humid, floral night air.

Len became aware of Danon, who was watching him watch Albigard. He shook himself loose from his preoccupation, and instead turned his attention to stripping off his filthy clothes. Once again, Len marveled at the idea that not so long ago, he'd taken access to daily showers with soap and shampoo and conditioner for granted.

Also, washing machines. It was frankly amazing how little appreciation modern humans gave washing machines.

Naked, he stepped into the steaming pool with a hiss of pleasure. His skin above the waterline erupted into gooseflesh, only to flush with heat as he sank in deeper. A delicious feeling of warmth soaked into his muscles and bones within moments. He groaned and opened his eyes, only to find Albigard staring at him every bit as fixedly as Len had been staring at Albigard earlier.

Their eyes locked.

Danon chuckled. "The gossip about you two was right, I see. A human and a Fae, who'd've thought?"

Wait. There was gossip about them *already*? Apparently, Leesa had been busy since their little talk that afternoon. Len raised his eyebrows, but the horrible specter of *tomorrow* hanging over their

heads had also brought out a certain kind of reck-
lessness in him.

"Well, he might be a Fae, but nobody's perfect," he managed in a casual tone. "And besides — I
mean... *look* at him."

Another chuckle. "Aye, he's a pretty one, and
no mistake... if your tastes run that way."

Albigard, meanwhile, had a bit of a *deer-in-the-
headlights* thing going on.

Danon hauled himself out of the water, revealing mountains of muscle and a flaccid dick that
could choke a horse. "Suppose I'll leave you to it,
then. If you need anything, there's a shelf carved
into the wall at the top of the path. There's water
gourds if you get thirsty, and oil if... well, you
know. Our place is yours, and all that." He
stretched and gave a mighty yawn. "Tomorrow is
another realm."

"Thanks," Len said faintly, as the hulking Fae
pulled on his simple clothing and brushed past Albigard with a comradely pat to his shoulder.
Albigard still stood frozen, blinking after him.

NINE

Once Danon was out of earshot, Albigard turned a bewildered gaze on Len. "Did he just…?"

"Yeah, I'm pretty sure he did." Len scrubbed a hand through his messy hair. "Welcome to the land of the liberal hippy Fae, where they don't seem to care if men fuck men or women fuck women. They only care that everyone involved is an adult." He took a few cautious steps across the pool and sank onto a convenient stone ledge that ran around the side like a bench. Leaning back until the water lapped at his collarbones, he waved a hand at Albigard. "So… go on, then. Less talking. More stripping."

Tomorrow is another realm.

Maybe if Len repeated it in his head enough times, he'd start to believe it.

Albigard absently laid the parcel of food on a rock next to the pool and started on the fastenings of his brocade tunic. He appeared deep in thought as his fingers slid the silk laces through one set of grommets after another. Len — still in serious need of distraction — settled in to watch the show.

It was clear Albigard's mind wasn't on what he was doing, but he slid out of his tunic and linen undershirt, pulled off his tall boots, and peeled himself out of his tight leather trousers efficiently enough. The shifting shadows cast by the sprites kept Len from looking his fill as much as he might have liked, and then Albigard was stepping into the pool with him. He settled in, mirroring Len's position on the other side, and let his head fall back to rest on the edge. Len stared at the exposed line of a long, pale throat.

Tomorrow is another realm.

He repeated the silent mantra a bit desperately.

After a few moments, Albigard lifted his head, an intent expression lining his face. "How are you?"

Right. Because Len had already admitted to not being okay. He closed his eyes, trying to put all the unraveling parts of himself back where they belonged for a few more hours.

"That depends," he said, "on whether I can keep my brain firmly focused on tonight, or whether it gets away from me and starts wandering toward tomorrow."

He heard Albigard take a breath and hold it, as though he was working up to something. "Is that a request for a few hours of escape into a different role? One where you have more... control of events?"

Len opened his eyes abruptly.

"Would you like it to be?" he asked in a cautious tone.

But Albigard's intent look didn't waver. "The question is, would *you* like it to be?"

Len held out for maybe five seconds before he broke. "Yes. Oh, god, yes please." He swallowed, and made himself run through practical considerations. "Other people from the camp might show up, though. They don't care if we have sex here, but would it bother you?"

For his part, Albigard did appear to give the matter serious consideration. "I'm not entirely certain. It isn't something that's really come up before."

Len nodded, appreciating the honesty. "I can keep half an eye on the entrance. Tell you if someone else shows up? And the safewords — red or yellow — would still apply."

Albigard mulled that for a few moments. "That should be sufficient." In a rare burst of humor, he added, "After all, it seems like a squandered opportunity to actually be among the Forsaken, and not take advantage of the opportunity."

Len welcomed the little bubble of amusement that shuddered free of his chest. "Not only inside the Forsaken camp, but *naked*, no less. How scandalous."

"Just so."

Perhaps unsurprisingly, Albigard seemed at a bit of a loss as to what to do now that he'd taken the initiative and started them down this road. Len felt some of the tension in his neck begin to unknot, and it wasn't just due to the pool's soothing heat.

"Go get us some water from the shelf Danon told us about," Len ordered. "Bring it to me, along with the food they gave you, and the energy bar that's in my jeans pocket."

Albigard levered himself out of the pool without complaint to do as he was asked, water sluicing along lean planes of muscle. Len watched him the whole way as he climbed higher along the path and examined the contents of the recessed storage area near the top.

Tomorrow is another realm.

Tomorrow is another realm, damn it. Only tonight matters.

The Fae returned with a water gourd, descending the rocky path with effortless grace. He crouched to retrieve the other items Len had requested. Reentering the pool, he carried everything to Len's side, where he arranged the little pile of food and drink on the edge beside him, within easy reach.

"Well done, princeling," Len told him. "Hmm... you know, you're turning out to be more trainable than I originally thought." He reached for the energy bar and peeled open the wrapper, using it to gesture to the water in front of him. "Now, hands behind your back. Hold your left wrist with your right hand, and kneel right here until I need you again."

Albigard hesitated.

Len quirked an eyebrow. "No? Looks like I spoke too soon," he said, and set the energy bar aside. He stood up and pressed into Albigard's space, chest to chest, reaching around to tangle a fistful of Albigard's extravagant mane of hair in his fingers—using the grip to tilt his head back. "How disappointing. Do I need to explain the phrases 'hands behind your back' and 'kneel until I need you' in greater detail, princeling?"

He kept his tone conversational, watching Albigard's eyes carefully. Albigard gave a fitful little jerk against Len's hold on his hair, and Len pulled his head back another inch. They stared at each other for a breathless moment... and Albigard closed his eyes, folding at the knees.

Len kept his grip as Albigard went down, relishing the Fae's sharp gasp of surprise when the water sloshed around his chin, deeper than he'd bargained for. Len steadied him, stepping behind him and releasing his hold in favor of running his hands down Albigard's arms and guiding them behind his back. When he let go, Albigard kept them where Len had put them.

"*Much* better." Len left him there, balanced on his knees with his head tilted back to keep his face out of the water, and returned to his seat. He picked up his energy bar and ate it slowly, listening to the hitch of his companion's uneven breathing.

When he was done, he set the empty wrapper aside and reached for the container of water. "Since this is communal, can I drink it safely? It wouldn't be considered a gift?"

"No. It would not be considered a gift," Albigard said, sounding a bit strained.

"Great." Len uncorked it and raised it to his lips, slaking his thirst. When he was done, he closed it and set it aside. He rose, walking in a tight circle around Albigard, who jerked his chin higher to avoid the little waves the movement caused.

Stopping at the Fae's back, he looped a hand loosely around Albigard's throat and used it to tug him backward to lean against Len's body. Albigard tensed and gasped at the loss of balance, only to relax against the support a few heartbeats later. The back of his head rested against Len's stomach.

"I've been thinking about what I should do with you now that you're a prisoner here, princeling," Len said. "It occurred to me that I could just keep you here in the baths permanently — chain you to the wall with an ankle shackle, and make you a fuckable part of the scenery. What do you think?"

Albigard didn't answer, but he didn't need to. The way his pulse picked up beneath Len's fingers answered for him.

"I think you'd secretly love that, wouldn't you?" Len went on, stroking upward to slide wet fingertips over Albigard's parted lips. "No responsibilities beyond pleasuring anyone who wants to use your body... no control over what they do to you. You could just lounge around all day in this beautiful place. People would bring you food to eat and wine to drink... keep you bathed and pampered between fucking."

The breath caressing Len's fingertips was ragged.

"As you say, I am your prisoner," Albigard managed. "If you choose to degrade me in such a way, it's not as though I can stop you."

"That's right," Len agreed easily. "I imagine you'd be in high demand, too. I picture members of the camp lining up to use you — over and over, not stopping even when you pass out from coming so many times."

A rough tremor shuddered through the body pressed against his. Len lowered himself in the water until he could reach around and grope between the Fae's legs, careful to keep supporting Albigard's weight as he did so.

The noise Albigard made when Len's hand closed around an erection that felt almost painfully hard was enough to have Len's dick straining to alertness in response. Len pumped the Fae a few times and let go, leaving him panting. He wrapped his arm around Albigard's chest and dragged him upright so they were both standing. The maneuver maybe wasn't as graceful as he'd pictured—but at least neither of them ended up slipping and getting unceremoniously dunked.

"Sit on the bench." Len turned Albigard in his arms and walked him backward, pushing him to sit in the spot Len had recently vacated. Len guided the Fae's hands up and out of the water, placing them on a convenient shelf of rock jutting out from the wall about a foot above his head. "Your wrists are magically bound to this rock now," he told his captive. "Don't try to struggle; you won't be able to get free."

Albigard's forest-colored eyes were all pupil in the shifting light from the sprites. His fingers curled around the edge of the natural outcropping of stone.

"What will you do to me, now that you have me trapped?" he murmured.

Len rested a knee on the bench next to Albigard's hard-muscled thigh, half-straddling him as he reached for the parcel of food the others had sent with him. He opened it, finding a mix of fresh berries and cubes of cooked meat inside. With a challenging look, he picked up a berry and brushed it against Albigard's lips.

"I haven't decided yet," he said. "But whatever it is, you'll probably need a fair amount of energy for it. Gotta keep the blood sugar up, after all."

Albigard stretched forward to nip the berry from Len's fingers, and Len was instantly hard as a damned rock. He blinked, a bit dazed by the combination of heat from the water and the abrupt southerly migration of his blood flow.

Well, hello, previously undiscovered kink, he thought, and clawed back enough of his wits to reach for a morsel of meat.

He fed Albigard the entire contents of the leaf-wrapped package, ignoring the increasingly urgent throb of his cock as the Fae bastard started licking the juice from his fingers, pulling them between his lips to lave at the tips with every new offering.

"If I didn't know better," Len said, when the last bite had been swallowed and chased down with a long drink of water, "I'd think you were silently begging me for something."

"I do not beg." The words were a whisper.

"Hmm. Not in the last twenty-four hours, maybe," Len retorted, and reached between them to jerk Albigard's cock beneath the water until the Fae was writhing beneath him. He let go when it started to swell and throb in his hand, and Albigard entirely failed to swallow the noise of frustrated desire that rose from the back of his throat at the loss.

Len waited until he'd calmed down a bit, then hitched his hips forward a few inches so their dicks brushed, fencing with each other. Albigard drew in a sharp breath.

"Problem?" Len asked mildly.

The Fae clenched his jaw and did not answer, though his hips rolled, thrusting ineffectually in search of friction. Len smiled sweetly at him and slid a hand down his tattooed chest, teasing first one nipple and then the other into taut peaks beneath the surface. Albigard's head fell back, and he let out a soft moan.

Len tortured the hard nubs with deliberate and dedicated attention as he narrated every filthy idea that came into his head regarding all the things that could be done to someone chained up for public use in a communal bath. The Fae bucked and squirmed beneath him, stealing Len's breath every time their erections ground together.

"I..." Albigard gasped, about thirty seconds before Len would have given in and finished them both off without further prompting. "Please... I need..."

Len wrapped a hand around both of their dicks and pumped.

"What you need is a solid thousand years of fucking to make up for lost time," he panted. "Everyone can see it. Danon saw it. He thought you were pretty... he probably went back to the cave to get a bunch of his buddies. Maybe he's bringing them here right now to take turns with you once I'm finished."

Albigard made a tortured sound and convulsed, his knuckles white on the ledge he was grasping as he came explosively beneath Len—an expression like that of a martyred saint twisting his perfect features.

Len's orgasm crashed over him in response to the sight laid out before him, his vision tunneling for the space of a few heartbeats before oxygen returned to his brain and left him gasping. He slumped against the shuddering form beneath him, waiting for his muscles to start responding again, his breath damp against Albigard's neck in the humid air.

Tears prickled at the corners of his eyes.

Tomorrow is another realm.

And he *couldn't* fall apart right now. He was still domming... still responsible for another's physical and emotional wellbeing. Len swallowed hard and took his own weight, lifting himself off of the Fae's body.

"You were perfect, princeling," he whispered, stroking Albigard's cheek. "Absolutely perfect. Come here... drink some more water for me, and we'll get you freed so you can rest for a bit."

Len held the water so Albigard could drink, and then took his own advice and finished what was left in the gourd. One at a time, he eased Albigard's hands away from the rock he'd been clutching, and massaged the joints before settling them in the Fae's lap.

Albigard remained dazed and pliant beneath his care, floating along happily in subspace. He allowed Len to urge him out of the pool and onto a moss-covered rock, where he sat while Len climbed up to the storage shelf. There, he found a pile of thick furs presumably meant for drying off, or maybe for sitting on. Len returned to the Fae's side and laid out the furs on a flat stretch of moss-cushioned ground.

"Come here, princeling," he murmured, and guided Albigard to lie on his side in the warm night air. When he was comfortably settled, Len spooned him from behind, one arm wrapped protectively around his middle.

The Fae was asleep within moments. Len pressed his face into the nape of Albigard's neck, and tried to believe that the sun would never rise again.

TEN

When Len opened his eyes the following morning, the cat-sidhe was sitting cross-legged on the nearby rock, watching the pair of them with an expression of sad acceptance. The marks on their face and throat had faded to pink, except for one particularly bad bruise that was still mottled yellow and green.

Len carefully untangled himself from Albigard, who slept on, oblivious. His conspicuous nudity would normally have been the most immediate issue on Len's mind... but the sight of the elfin figure brought everything else crashing into him like a derailed freight train. Compared to the realization that the Hunt had been roaming freely on Earth for more than a day, and he was now expected to shuffle Albigard off to his death at the hands of every Fae's childhood nightmare, the fact that his dick was hanging out didn't really rate.

"What happened to his magic?" the sidhe asked quietly. "I sensed its absence yesterday."

A lump rose in Len's throat, and he had to force the words out. "He lied to protect me from his father."

The cat-sidhe nodded. "I see."

"That's it?" Len demanded, bitterness clawing its way up from his stomach. "No words of profound sidhe wisdom? No moral judgments?"

"No," said the little Fae. "It will not affect the outcome of what we must do today. In the end, it does not matter."

Len's temper boiled over, and he directed it at the only convenient target. "Yes it fucking matters!" he snapped, barely remembering to keep his voice down. "It matters that he's getting punished for trying keep someone else safe! It matters that we're using him as *bait* for this thing!"

He leaned forward, tangling his fingers in his fringe of blue hair. Only then did he become aware of how badly his hands were shaking.

"Of course you are right, human," the sidhe said in a soothing tone. The words sounded genuine. "Forgive me. I spoke thoughtlessly."

Len tried to breathe against the hitch in his chest. "I don't think I can do this." His voice broke on the words.

A warm hand closed on his forearm.

"You must," Albigard said, a sleepy, early morning rasp. "*We* must. Both our worlds hang in the balance."

"I know," Len said miserably, not uncurling. "I know that."

Everyone on Earth was depending on them to walk into the lion's den, where Albigard would sacrifice himself to the one thing he feared most. Len might or might not survive that endgame. He was a side character... a nameless bodyguard meant to help deliver Albigard to his appointment with fate, and keep him from getting eaten at the wrong time or in the wrong place.

His stomach churned.

The hand on his arm squeezed. "Come," Albigard said. "The sooner we leave, the better."

"You should eat something first," Len said reflexively, since caretaking other people had always been one of his coping mechanisms.

"So should you," Albigard retorted.

But honestly, dumping food on his roiling stomach was the very last thing on Len's mind at that moment.

"Let us depart now," said the cat-sidhe. "I have acquired weapons for the journey. Your Unseelie may hunt breakfast for us as we travel, human. That way, you need have no worries about accepting the food."

Len straightened with reluctance, scrubbing his hands over his face — pulling at his metal piercings with ruthless disregard, just to feel something that wasn't sick dread.

"I would enjoy that," Albigard said. "My most recent opportunity for hunting lacked much in the way of challenge."

With a sharp pang, Len remembered the fifteen-minute opossum expedition in suburban Chicago. His eyes moved listlessly over the items lying on the ground next to the cat-sidhe's perch. A bow and a quiver of arrows. Two leather belts with knife sheaths.

"Okay, fine. Let's go," he managed, because the only thing worse than what was about to happen would be if Albigard left without Len and went to his death alone... or if the Hunt showed up before they were ready for it.

The Fae handed Len his pile of rumpled designer clothes before reaching for his own clothing. "Has the Wild Hunt returned to Dhuinne yet?" Albigard asked the sidhe.

"No, not yet," the pixie-like figure replied. "The camp is packing up to leave as a precaution. I can portal the three of us to the edge of the protected zone around Chaima, but it will take us the better part of the day to penetrate the magical barrier."

Albigard nodded, accepting it. Len pulled on his clothing, relieved to find that his muscles were not as sore as he'd expected after yesterday's exertion. Albigard strapped on the weapons the sidhe had brought him, and handed the second knife belt to Len.

Len stared at it. "You realize I have no idea how to use this, right?" he asked. "My one and only experience with knife fighting ended up with me getting skewered through the lung. I'd prefer not to repeat that experience anytime soon."

A wan smile tugged at the corner of Albigard's lips. "Take it anyway. If nothing else, I'm sure you can use it to cut up meat for breakfast."

Len took the belt and strapped it over his hips, feeling vaguely ridiculous. With a final look around the unearthly beauty of the grotto, he gave himself a few self-indulgent moments to picture a world where he brought Albigard here every night and shattered the Fae with pleasure. His eyes slid closed.

"I'm still not ready for this," he told the others. "Can we please hurry up and go anyway?"

"Yes, human," said the cat-sidhe. "We will go now."

Len opened his eyes as a portal burned its way into existence in front of them. Albigard stepped through without hesitation. Len couldn't boast the same, but he made himself follow, unwilling to let Albigard out of his sight for more than a moment. The sidhe came through right after him, and the portal snapped shut.

They were in a forest, though like so much of Dhuinne, it was more of a jungle.

"Another good use for a knife," Albigard observed dryly, taking in the tangle of overgrown paths around them.

"Yes," agreed the cat-sidhe. "This journey would, in fact, be considerably easier were it not for the very problem we are here to address."

Len looked up, taking in the towering deciduous trees. "Is one of these Chaima?"

"No, human," said the sidhe. "Chaima is the *world*-tree. It dwarfs these tiny things."

"Umm..." Len said. "Okay. So, how do we get there, exactly?"

"The tree exists inside a fold in space, I suppose you might say." The cat-sidhe turned in a slow circle, examining their surroundings. "We must complete a full circuit around the circumference of the protected area. Once I have charted its boundaries, I will be able to see inside."

Len looked at Albigard. "Does that make sense to you, I hope?"

"It does. Think of it like the recursive bound-ary layer that surrounded the pocket realm," Albigard said. "You charted one edge of it. If you had followed it all the way around, you would have understood the shape of the interior. This situation is, I gather, somewhat the reverse."

Len thought about that. "Right. If I ignore eve-rything I thought I knew about how reality works, I guess that makes sense."

Albigard shrugged. "Humans are not exactly renowned throughout the three realms for under-standing how reality works."

The cat-sidhe gave a small snort. "We should get a start on things—the journey is likely to be several leagues' travel. I will gather berries if you will hunt, Unseelie, and we will stop for a meal once we acquire enough food for one."

Without waiting for a response, the sidhe headed off in what seemed like an arbitrary direc-tion. For the most part, they were able to squeeze through gaps in the vines and brush, though occa-sionally one of them had to hack a larger opening through the plant life.

When Len detoured around a patch of vines that his more graceful companions had slipped through, he found the edge of the fold in space. Just as it had in the pocket realm, his path twisted in a different direction than the one his feet had been pointed toward. He realized with a chill that left to his own devices, he'd get hopelessly turned around and lost before he'd gone a hundred feet.

This, apparently, was the sidhe's special skill. They could sense the edge of the boundary without getting disoriented by it. For his part, Albigard seemed to be watching the cat-sidhe, rather than their surroundings, to gauge their path. Even so, when he darted off in pursuit of a rustle in the underbrush, bow drawn, Len felt a moment of panic.

"Will he be able to find his way back in this weirdness?" he whispered urgently.

The sidhe paused to pick a handful of red berries from a low tree branch, adding them to a pouch hanging at their waist. "Yes, but we will wait here to make it easier for him."

Indeed, Albigard returned a few minutes later. He was empty-handed, but Len couldn't help his sigh of relief. Twice more, the Fae disappeared into the confusion of trees, and they stopped to wait for him. On his third expedition, a high-pitched squeal emerged from the bushes. Shortly afterward, he reappeared with a creature about the size of a very large rabbit, but with small, round ears and a flat, paddle-shaped tail.

"Quickly." Albigard gestured to Len to approach.

He did, and saw with an unpleasantly queasy sensation that the mystery animal was still alive, its chest rising and falling in rapid panting despite the arrow lodged in its flank. "It's not dead," he pointed out.

"I'm aware," Albigard told him. "And no — before you ask, this is not my preferred method to dispatch prey." With Len standing a step away, he crouched and placed the injured animal on the ground before cutting off its head with the blade of his dagger. Blood gushed, and Len drew in a sharp gasp as a chilly breath of... *something*... sank into him.

"Fascinating," said the cat-sidhe, who had been watching the proceedings with interest.

Len—who generally didn't have to deal with his meat until after it was already dead—still felt faintly ill.

"Did it work?" Albigard asked.

Nose-to-tail eating, Len reminded himself. *Nothing going to waste.*

"Yeah," he said. "It worked."

"There is a stream in this direction," the sidhe declared, heading down a partly overgrown animal trail. "We will build a fire on the bank, and eat."

They made their way down a gentle slope to the promised waterway. Albigard gathered dry wood while Len skinned and gutted the mystery critter with less skill than he would have liked. Some of the meat was fouled by the contents of the intestines, which had been pierced by the arrow. Len detached the shoulders and haunches, and filleted out the loin muscles, figuring that would still be plenty to feed three people.

The sidhe efficiently stripped the bark from a couple of green branches with forked ends, and had Len thread the meat onto a third stick with a sharpened point. Albigard came back with wood for a fire, and cleared the vines from a section of the pebbled bank. The sidhe started the fire with magic, and soon had it blazing merrily away—the forked sticks stuck in the ground on either side to act as support for the spitted meat.

Len babysat their meal, turning it every couple of minutes to roast it evenly. While he was cooking the meat, Albigard brought him a waxy, tubular leaf filled with water from the stream, and Len ended up spilling half of it down his chin because drinking from a leaf wasn't nearly as easy as it sounded. When the meat was cooked, they ate. There was no seasoning—nothing except the char from the fire. It was still amazing, and Len once more felt the tingle of disquiet over how unnaturally *good* everything tasted in this realm.

The water was sweet. The berries were tangy. The mystery critter was more succulent than the best prime rib Len had ever eaten.

To distract himself, he turned to the cat-sidhe and raised a subject that had been bothering him. "There was a cu-sidhe guarding you when we got you out of that vault where Oren was keeping you."

"Was there?" asked the sidhe.

"Yeah," Len confirmed. "Shouldn't the cu-sidhe be on your side? Why would they help Oren?"

The diminutive Fae gave a mirthless smile. "Unfortunately, the cu-sidhe tend to go where they are led. It's something of a characteristic of theirs."

"If Oren told them that it was necessary to keep the cat-sidhe safely out of the way until they'd used me to bring the Hunt to heel in Dhuinne," Albigard added, "I'm sure they would have done so without question."

From what he'd seen of the dog-like Fae, Len supposed it made sense.

"Are Oren and the Court likely to realize that we've come here?" Len wondered. "To Chaima, I mean."

"Unlikely," said the cat-sidhe. "They still seem to be laboring under the misapprehension that luring the Hunt back to Dhuinne and allowing it to consume its prey will be sufficient to bring it back under their control. *Fools.*"

"What do you think is really causing this... imbalance in Dhuinne?" Len asked. "If it's not the Hunt, I mean?"

The cat-sidhe looked pensive. "If I knew that, human, we would not be in this situation in first place."

"It all started soon after the war ended," Albigard put in. "Perhaps the demons used some kind of weapon we do not know about, causing damage to the veil and throwing things out of alignment."

"Perhaps," said the cat-sidhe, though they didn't sound convinced.

The three of them finished eating and extinguished the fire, throwing water on it to prevent any possibility of embers. The cat-sidhe retraced their path, leading them back to the exact spot where they'd detoured from the edge of the fold in reality for their meal. Their little group continued at a steady pace, hacking a trail through the jungle-like forest until Len was exhausted and sore, with fresh blisters on both heels complaining at every step.

The sun had risen to its zenith in the lavender sky and gotten a good start on its afternoon descent by the time the sidhe finally called a halt. "Here we are."

Len couldn't see anything familiar about their surroundings at first, but then he looked down and saw footprints in the damp loam. One set had the distinctive tread of Doc Martens.

They had arrived back at their starting point.

The cat-sidhe peered intently into the area of jungle they'd just circumnavigated. "Yes, I see it now. Come, my friends."

With a gesture of one hand, the little Fae called up a portal. Rather than murky darkness, a luminous golden glow emanated from the center. Albigard straightened his spine and stepped through, his chin held high. Len swallowed against the hollow ache in his stomach and followed.

On the other side, he was confronted with a tree so massive that it took up the entire sky.

ELEVEN

The cat-sidhe followed them through and closed the portal. Len tried to take everything in, but it didn't work. This appeared to be another one of those things human brains simply weren't designed to process.

They were still quite a distance from the tree... or at least, he *thought* they were. It was so big that it messed with his perception of scale. The impression that it took up all the available space was further reinforced by the nebulous nature of the rest of their surroundings. Everything was misty, illuminated by the diffuse, golden glow he'd seen through the portal.

There was no sign of the choking jungle-forest they'd just left. If pressed, Len would have said the world tree was set in endless, rolling grassland, but any attempt to look at the actual grass just sort of... slid away, not sticking in his awareness.

One thing was clear enough, though — the tree was damaged. The trunk tilted at a slight angle... and not the dramatic sort of natural angle that some trees took on in response to being shaped by the wind. This was a straight tree whose root system was beginning to give way. From their slightly elevated vantage point on a hill, they could see where the ground around one side of the tree had heaved upward, exposing torn roots.

"Oh, no," said the cat-sidhe, looking at the massive, damaged monument with genuine distress. "No, this is *very bad*."

Len's insides twisted when he tried to picture what might happen if the tree ever fell. Would it take all of Dhuinne with it? Would it take *everything* with it? His breath caught.

Beside him, Albigard appeared dazed. For lack of any better ideas, Len reached out and tangled their fingers together, as Albigard had done when Len learned that the Hunt might well be rampaging through populated areas back on Earth.

"We'll fix it," he told the Fae a bit desperately. "We're going to fix it, okay? It's going to be all right."

Albigard blinked free of his reverie and swallowed. His lips parted, but no words emerged.

"We must not tarry," the cat-sidhe said. "The Hunt returned to Dhuinne while we were traveling. I can sense its approach."

Len jerked his head around. "*What*? You might have mentioned that earlier!"

"There is still time," said the sidhe. "It seemed pointless to alarm you with something over which we have no control. Hurry, now. Let us find a way into the caverns beneath the tree."

Albigard started toward Chaima without a word, like someone moving inside a dream. Len only realized that their hands were still clasped when Albigard pulled his away. The sick, panicked feeling that had been thrumming beneath Len's skin ever since he'd awoken that morning ratcheted up another notch.

They headed toward the damaged area where some of the roots had been torn up, speeding to a jog when the cat-sidhe pointed out a dark gap among the confusion of rock and earth. It took longer to get to it than Len would have predicted, and when they did, his brain balked abruptly at the scope of the tree looming above him. It was as though a skyscraper had grown branches and taken over the world.

His blisters throbbed as he hobbled to a stop in front of the ominous gap in the ground. The cat-sidhe gestured them to stay back and ducked inside, disappearing for a few moments before reappearing.

"There is a pathway down to the main root structure," the little Fae said tersely. "And sprites have taken up residence inside. There is enough light to see."

Albigard nodded, his face pale in the golden light. "The Hunt?"

"Getting closer." The cat-sidhe turned to Len. "Human... you need not go inside with him. You have already done more than could be asked of an outworlder."

Len tried to think past his thundering pulse and the nausea coiling in his gut. "I'm going with him." The words emerged unsteady despite his best efforts.

"You do not need to—" Albigard began.

"*I'm going with you!*" He barely recognized his own voice.

Albigard closed his mouth. His expression was haggard. Instead, he turned to the cat-sidhe. "I have only one further request, Elder. I don't claim to understand the nature of your connection with the demon Nigellus. But if the Hunt is successfully contained and it is possible to allow him passage to Dhuinne under flag of truce, please try to arrange it. He believes it may still be possible to retrieve the souls of Ransley Thorpe and Zorah Bright from the Void, using the Hunt as a conduit. If it is, I beg you to assist him in doing so."

The cat-sidhe's expression grew achingly sad. "If it is within my power, I will try to make it so, *a leanbh*. But if the Hunt is truly absorbed back into Mother Dhuinne, it may not be possible."

Len wanted to shout in frustration... to take the sidhe by the shoulders and shake them. *Couldn't you at least let him have this one hope to hold on to?* he wanted to demand. *Couldn't you use that Fae gift for talking circles around a lie, and let him have this one damned thing?*

It wasn't the cat-sidhe's fault, though. He knew that. None of this was the fault of anyone here. Aside from the Forsaken, the three of them were the only ones on Dhuinne who'd been willing to try and fix things before they careened completely out of control.

But it wasn't *fair*.

"I understand," Albigard said hoarsely. "Your assistance in this matter has been greatly appreciated."

Len probably should have said something as well... thanked the sidhe for helping Len find Albigard and free him before his father's henchmen succeeded in throwing him into Hell, if nothing else. But if he opened his mouth, he wasn't sure what was going to come out of it, so he kept his jaw clamped tightly shut.

The cat-sidhe reached up and urged Albigard to lower his head to their height, placing a chaste kiss upon his brow when he complied. "Go with Dhuinne's blessing, Albigard of the Unseelie. May your soul find peace among Chaima's leaves and branches."

The air rasped in Len's throat, hot and painful as he held back the awful, burgeoning knot of grief and rage that wanted to break free. He couldn't let it get out. Not yet. Not when it would only make Albigard feel worse. But when that burning ball of emotion finally did escape his control — and it would — Len wasn't sure there was going to be anything left of him afterward.

"Go, quickly," the sidhe said, releasing Albigard. "There is little time left."

"You'll be safe here?" Albigard asked.

"Yes, I will stay out of harm's way." Catlike green eyes met Len's burning ones. "When it is done, I will be waiting nearby."

... *if you survive* remained unsaid, but Len heard it all the same.

He made himself turn to face Albigard, who studied him intently.

"You are certain you wish to come?" the Fae asked him.

Len managed a tight nod, still unable to speak. He turned toward the rip in the ground and started walking, aware of Albigard keeping pace at his shoulder. The opening in the ground was large enough for them to enter one at a time without having to stoop, but the footing was a tumble of stones and disturbed clods of dirt. After the first few feet, it angled sharply downward. It would have been a terrifying black maw, if not for the sprites that had taken up residence among the broken roots forming the walls and ceiling.

All right... it was *still* a terrifying maw leading to unknown danger. But at least the cheerfully twinkling lights meant they could see their way down to Albigard's doom.

Len skidded on loose rocks and had to accept a steadying hand from the Fae, whose preternatural grace still persisted, even in the absence of his magic. Eventually, the ground beneath their feet evened out somewhat, the space around them opening into a cavern many times larger than the cave where the Forsaken had based their camp.

Len looked around, taking in the massive, twisting roots embedded in the walls. "Why is there a cavern like this beneath a tree?" he asked in a rasping voice. "Why isn't it just solid dirt and rock?"

Albigard sounded remote, as though he were already distancing himself from what was about to happen to him. "In the stories, it is because the roots are a conduit of destructive elemental magic. They have been absorbing the rock and soil since the beginning of time, using it to grow the trunk and branches. The caverns are the places they have already eaten away."

Len wanted to reply to that, to keep the conversation going and provide some sort of distraction from the reality closing in around them. Somehow, he couldn't seem to manage it.

"One wonders if the growing dead spaces are responsible for the instability we saw above," Albigard continued absently.

"No, that's not it," Len said, the words leaving his lips before his brain even registered them. He frowned, chasing something at the edges of his awareness, but it was already gone.

"Oh?" Albigard asked. "You have another theory?"

Len opened his mouth and paused. "No, I..." He trailed off, shaking his head. "Sorry. I don't know why I said that."

"We're both a bit distracted at present, I think," Albigard replied, reaching for humor and falling well short.

They continued deeper into the underground space, neither of them entirely sure what to do beyond waiting for the Hunt to show up. Len berated himself for being on the verge of falling apart when he wasn't even the one being asked to make the sacrifice.

But what were you supposed to say to someone walking to the gallows? How did you make it better *when there was no conceivable way to make it better*?

"This sucks," he choked out. Which... *yeah*. Was basically the opposite of making things better.

Albigard hesitated, his footsteps slowing.

"I find the current situation preferable to any alternative in which the Hunt catches up to me, only to continue its uncontrolled rampage across the realms afterward." The Fae's voice was calm, but he still sounded distant.

"I know," Len managed. "But it sucks, even so."

Albigard tilted his head, an acknowledgement of sorts. His gaze roamed around the cavern. "If it helps, I imagine very few people have ever seen this place—seen Chaima up close, and walked among its roots. You are almost certainly the first human to do so." He wandered forward, lifting a hand to the twisted mass of roots weaving through the wall. "It is an undeniable honor. I only wish I was still in a position to sense its magic directly."

A tendril of root snaked out and wrapped around his wrist.

Len's eyes widened, and Albigard inhaled sharply in surprise. He tugged against the unexpected restraint, which held fast. Len was already halfway to his side when he threw up his other hand and snapped, "Stay back!"

"*Fuck that,*" Len snarled, without a second's thought. His hands closed over Albigard's forearm, adding his strength to the Fae's—but it was like pulling against steel. Even as they struggled against the living constraint, more roots wriggled out from the wall and floor. They ignored Len completely in favor of twisting around Albigard's arms and legs, dragging him down and covering more and more of his body as they thickened and hardened into impenetrable coils.

"*No, goddamn it!*" Len shouted, scrabbling for the knife at his belt and yanking it free of its sheath. He fell to his knees and started hacking at the thickest of the roots, but the iron blade might as well have been sawing away at solid stone. "Albigard—"

The Fae had ceased struggling. His green eyes slid past Len's shoulder, and a single shudder went through him.

"Stop," he said in an unnaturally calm voice. "It doesn't matter now. Save your strength."

A horrible clammy feeling slid over Len's skin, and he turned to look behind him in the sickening knowledge of what he would find. Around the cavern, the sprites were swirling madly, as though panicked by the approach of a predator. Beyond, oily black smoke rolled down through the tunnel leading from the surface, extinguishing their tiny, twinkling lights one by one.

TWELVE

Len couldn't hold back the low, wordless noise of denial that escaped his throat as the Wild Hunt spilled into Chaima's underground cavern.

In his twisted coffin of roots, Albigard closed his eyes for a long moment before opening them again. Len crouched over him protectively, knowing it was hopeless... knowing that even if he could somehow save him from the Hunt, by doing so he would be condemning both their worlds to a slow and painful death.

"If..." Albigard's voice was a barely audible rasp. He swallowed and tried again. "If Nigellus is successful in retrieving them, tell Thorpe and the demonkin not to mourn me. Tell them I'm sorry... for all of it."

Burning fear and frustration welled up behind Len's eyes and spilled over, trailing salt water down his cheeks. "I'll tell them," he promised, cupping Albigard's jaw in his palm. "They'll understand, I promise."

The Fae looked up at him with luminous eyes, as more and more of the sprites winked out. "Tears, *a rúnsearc*? Do not weep for me. Only..."

"What?" Len asked. "Just ask... I'll do anything. I'm *sorry*. I'm so sorry —"

"Don't leave me," Albigard murmured, a quiet plea.

Len swallowed a sob and leaned forward the last few inches, brushing his lips against the Fae's in a tender kiss, just as the last of the twinkling lights extinguished. For an endless moment, Albigard's lips moved against his, catching lightly against Len's piercing—warm and alive and real in the darkness, even as the clammy chill of the Hunt rolled over them.

Between one heartbeat and the next, those warm lips went slack as the life fled Albigard's body on a breath, leaving only a cold and empty shell behind. Len knelt in the dark, feeling as though his heart had just been ripped out. The Wild Hunt howled in triumph, swirling around him without making contact—held back only by the tattered cloak of death surrounding him. Len's fingers tightened on the coils of root cocooning the Fae's lifeless body, his nails digging into the living wood. A noise as terrible as any the Hunt had ever made bubbled up from his chest, demanding release.

Beneath his grip, the roots grew warm, then hot. A golden glow cut through the greasy darkness shrouding him, and he blinked rapidly as the roots began to move again—still ignoring him, but now coiling upward and outward, into the oily mass of the Wild Hunt. The glow increased until the roots almost seemed to become translucent, allowing Len to see as the Hunt's darkness was sucked into them and siphoned toward the main mass of the world tree.

He fell back on his heels, holding his breath as the Hunt began to howl again, perhaps sensing that it was about to be trapped. The noise thundered through Len's chest, more a feeling than an actual sound. An unnatural wind rose inside the cavern, ruffling his hair.

The eerie light spread through the cavern, more roots coming to life and grasping at the Hunt with every second that passed. The winds rose to a gale; the howling grew in pitch until it rattled Len's bones.

All at once, the Hunt ripped free of the roots surrounding Albigard, opening a larger bubble of space around Len. He scrambled to his feet on shaking legs, watching in disbelief as the roiling mass of darkness tore itself loose and began to retreat toward the tunnel to the surface, still wailing like a banshee.

"No..." Len breathed, suddenly, agonizingly aware that he was the only one who could possibly block the Hunt's escape through the narrow entrance to the outside world, and he'd been kneeling over a corpse instead of getting in a position to *do the one damn thing he was here to do.*

Panic beat at Len's chest as he gauged the speed at which the Hunt was tearing itself free of Chaima's grasping roots, versus the distance separating him from the entrance to the vast underground gallery. The impossibility of it sliced him to the bone. He stumbled forward, the glow of the roots' magic illuminating the roiling black mass as its far edge reached the bottom of the tunnel.

"No," he breathed again, as the prospect of having sacrificed Albigard for *nothing* flooded through his chest like frigid, brackish water.

Rage followed close on its heels. Icy, crackling rage, the likes of which he'd never felt in his entire twenty-eight years of existence. The absolute, immovable need to be at the other end of the cavern *right the fuck now* grabbed Len's heart in a vise and *squeezed*.

A cold and terrible power rose from somewhere deep within him, demanding its release.

He lifted a hand, his fingers curling into claws. "No you *fucking don't*!" he shouted, the volume of the words rising until it was a roar—a denial that would twist reality itself before admitting defeat to this horrible, sickening *thing*.

Crackling energy sank into his skin and exploded outward from his raised hand, rippling along the length of the underground cavern like blue flames. It rushed past the retreating bulk of the Hunt, careening into the unstable tunnel leading to the surface, which groaned and collapsed in an explosion of rock, dirt, and dust.

Blocking the only exit.

Trapping the Hunt underground with Chaima's grasping roots... and with Len.

His knees abruptly stopped taking his weight, and he crumpled to the ground, half-sprawled across the tangle of roots encasing Albigard's body as the Hunt shrieked and wailed its rage around him. His vision wavered in and out, but he was dimly aware of more and more roots unfurling from the walls and floor, twisting into the mass of greasy smoke and sucking the Hunt's darkness into the world tree.

The Wild Hunt flailed and screamed, crashing over Len like a tsunami. It battered at him, kept at bay only by the remnants of flickering animus left over from a tiny, nameless animal's death—a last gift from Albigard, the creature sacrificed to Len's necromancy in hopes that the final boost of power would be useful to him during the struggle they all knew was coming.

Len clung to the coiling roots, his face resting inches from Albigard's with its staring, horror-filled green eyes. Tears trickled down Len's temple and the side of his nose as he lay exhausted and beaten, watching more and more of the Hunt disappear into Chaima's massive form.

He had no idea how long it took. But eventually, the wailing wind faded to a breeze, and then to nothing. The glow of the roots flared brighter as the last of the cancerous blackness flowed into them and disappeared. Then, the light faded by increments, pulsing like a heartbeat... and it was gone, leaving Len shuddering and unable to see, with only the corpse of his Fae lover for company.

In the end, it appeared he was destined to be alone in the dark after all.

THIRTEEN

He was cold. He was also fairly sure he should be feeling... *something.* Crippling grief? A sense of accomplishment at having achieved their goal? Fear of being trapped alone, underground?

Len lay still, draped across the roots covering Albigard's body and staring into nothing, too chilled by the death he'd channeled to even shiver.

It was the vague awareness of warmth kindling beneath his cheek and hands that finally succeeded in cutting through the heavy gray fog surrounding his thoughts. The roots began to glow again. With his face plastered against them and no strength to rise, Len was treated to an up-close and personal view as golden sparks trailed outward from the walls, traveling the same path as the oily darkness of the Hunt had when it was being absorbed, only in reverse.

The little sparks of light were pretty, he decided. Unfortunately, they also illuminated Albigard's haggard features and blank, staring eyes again—which Len really didn't like.

He should look away. It was hard, though. Even in death, Len wanted every last memory of the Fae he could get. And it helped that the diffuse golden glow lent a bit of color to his pallid cheeks. It softened the gaunt angles into something more lifelike... gave the illusion of a pink tinge to Albigard's perfect lips, rather than the ugly blue-gray of death.

Len stared at those lips for a while, remembering the way they'd felt beneath his. It had been their first kiss, he realized. Also, their last kiss.

When his gaze strayed back to Albigard's green eyes, the Fae's eyelids were closed.

Len blinked.

That... wasn't right. Was it?

The golden sparkles moving through the roots began to fade, but that same glow seemed to be coming from Albigard's skin now—a lucent aura spilling out from the Fae's body.

The roots slithered free from their death grip, like snakes wriggling away from prey they'd decided they didn't want. Len felt them retract beneath his limp body, squirming loose until he was lying across Albigard's torso directly, his left cheek pressed against dirty and rumpled silk brocade rather than fibrous wood. The glow dimmed gradually, until Len was once again in the dark.

He wanted to pretend that it was still last night, when he'd lain sated and tangled with Albigard on a pile of furs by the hot springs—because that fantasy was so much better than this reality. When a heartbeat thudded into existence beneath Len's ear, he decided that, yes, this was definitely turning into a nice hallucination. Maybe he would stay in it for a while.

The strangled gasp that expanded Albigard's lungs and nearly made Len slide right off his body seemed a bit much, to be honest. It sounded like someone surfacing from drowning, and wasn't really in the spirit of the comforting dream he was aiming for.

"What—?" a voice rasped. "*How...*"

Hands closed on Len's shoulders in the dark, manhandling him into a sitting position. His body lolled against the support, since he still had basically zero control of his own muscles. An arm closed around his back to steady him.

A new ball of light flared, making him wince at the sudden brightness. It floated upward, exactly like the balls of magical illumination Albigard used to be able to make, before he lost his magic while trying to keep Len safe. It lit the cavern, revealing the roots once more dormant in the walls and floor, as though nothing out of the ordinary had happened in the underground cavern at all.

"This is turning into a stupid dream," Len slurred.

A hand cupped his jaw, tilting his head up to meet the eyes of a ghost.

"The Hunt?" Albigard asked urgently.

"It killed you, and then it tried to get away, but I collapsed the tunnel entrance with blue magic and the tree ate it," Len said, feeling like he really shouldn't be forced to relive all this in the middle of his escapist hallucinatory fantasy.

"Can you walk?" the ghost demanded.

Len scoffed. "Does it look like I can walk?" he shot back. "Also, you're way more demanding than any of my other ghosts have been."

The ghost blinked at him. "I... daresay." Strong hands lowered him to lie on the floor, supporting his head on the way down. "Rest here. I will see what can be done about the tunnel entrance."

Panic speared Len's chest as the ghost made to rise. "*No!*" he gasped, lifting a numb hand. The movement lacked any kind of coordination, but it was still the first positive response his body had offered to his brain's commands. Fingers caught his, warm and alive and *oh god*, how Len wished this were real instead of his brain's pathetic attempt to dissociate from fresh trauma.

The ghost lifted his hand to warm lips, pressing a kiss to the knuckles before lowering it to rest on Len's chest. "You did not leave me alone," it said. "Trust that I will not leave you either, *a rúnsearc*. Only give me a few moments to see how we may best leave and rejoin the cat-sidhe. Perhaps they will be able to explain what has happened here."

Len still wanted this dream to return to their night by the hot springs, rather than... whatever the hell this was. He managed a small, reluctant nod. Fingers brushed his cheek, and Len let his eyes slip closed, since it was getting harder and harder to keep them open anyway.

After that, consciousness came in fits and starts. He was aware of being hefted over someone's shoulder—a fireman's carry that was super-uncomfortable and made him worry he might throw up. He was aware of the sound of crackling flames, and an abrupt feeling of disorientation that made the nausea even worse. He was aware of voices talking urgently, but not of what was said.

More crackling flames, more disorientation, and then he was being lowered onto something soft. A different kind of fire appeared in his hazy vision, tame and bounded by a ring of stones.

"I will check the food stores," said a familiar voice. *The cat-sidhe.* "You should both rest. Nothing will intrude here tonight. We will talk later."

A second voice answered, but Len was slipping again. He roused a bit when another body lay down next to him, a familiar sunlight-and-ozone scent tickling his nostrils. Len flopped toward it and clung, graceless and clumsy with exhaustion. Arms closed around him, a voice that no longer existed murmuring words in his ear that he couldn't understand.

It didn't matter. This was the hallucination Len had wanted all along—the one that would allow him to exist for a few more hours without his mind fracturing into a million razor-edged shards. He tightened numb fingers in silk brocade and let the darkness take him.

———————◆———————

Len woke alone some unknown amount of time later, not surprised by that fact in the least. Of course, lack of surprise did nothing to stop the awful sinking feeling that started in his stomach and spread outward to encompass his heart. Every beat of the damned thing felt like it was laboring against a cocoon of tightly wrapped barbed wire.

He swallowed, and swallowed again, hoping it might help. It didn't.

The campfire was still burning cheerfully inside its ring of stones. Familiar walls of stone surrounded him — the cave at the heart of the Forsaken camp. Someone had placed him on the pallet where Albigard had recovered after the loss of his magic, a mere couple of days ago. The blankets still smelled like him. The cavern was empty and echoing, its inhabitants gone. Len couldn't immediately tell if the Hunt had been through here or not.

Movement at the corner of his eye caught his attention. He managed to push himself partly upright, his body once more under his nominal control. The cat-sidhe sat cross-legged on the other side of the fire, sipping tea from a clay cup. Their expression was inscrutable, but some of the tension eased from their shoulders when Len rolled into a sitting position and rubbed at his face.

"You got me out of there," he said in a monotone, unsure exactly how he was supposed to feel about that fact.

The sidhe raised an elfin eyebrow at him.

"Not I, human," they said, and took another slow sip of tea.

Len stared blankly for a few seconds, trying to decide if he had the mental energy to pursue the conversation any further. He was leaning toward 'no' when a figure entered through the mouth of the cave. For a moment, all Len could process was the fact that the vines half-obscuring the opening were wilted and limp.

Then he took in the platinum hair pulled back in intricate braids, and the green silk tunic over black leather boots and breeches — clean and unmarked, as though they'd been put on fresh only recently. Len froze, blinking rapidly. The figure stayed solidly real.

"I was unable to find game or easy foraging in the immediate vicinity," Albigard said. "The Hunt has—" He cut himself off, his gaze falling on Len. "You're awake. Are you well?"

Len continued to stare. "But..." he said slowly. "That's... you're not..."

"I am not a specter, or a hallucination," Albigard told him. "You have my word on it—though perhaps such a declaration does not hold as much weight as it once did."

Len climbed to his feet, swaying a bit when his head protested the change in elevation. Albigard approached him cautiously, putting a hand out to steady him by an elbow.

The grip seemed real—skin on skin, warm and alive.

I felt you die, Len wanted to say. He couldn't though, because his lungs had seized at the first touch, and now they were working triple time... great, heaving gasps that did nothing to force back the dizziness making his vision waver.

Fingers cupped his cheek, and eyes the color of spring leaves filled Len's awareness, leaving room for nothing else.

"It would please me if you were calm," Albigard said in a low, resonant tone. "All is not well, but I am still with you. And, in fairness, things do seem considerably better now than they were a day ago."

Len choked on a sob of recognition, as his rampaging emotions yielded to a control not his own—the tension draining out of him and leaving him lightheaded. This was no ghost standing in front of him and manipulating his emotions... but a solid, living Albigard, flexing his magic like the entitled Fae asshole he was.

That trick had never worked very well on Len, and it took him only a moment to snap the control now. He reached a hand out to hook Albigard by the back of the neck and pull him forward until their foreheads rested together. His eyes slid closed as the most profound relief he'd ever felt in his life swept over him.

"How?" he whispered.

Albigard swallowed, his throat clicking. He made no move to pull away, speaking into their shared air.

"You would appear to have more insight into that question than I. My last memory is of asking you not to leave me... and your lips on mine." He took a deep, shuddering breath. "Then I woke up in the dark to find you collapsed across me, barely conscious. The tunnel leading into the underground cavern was blocked by debris and crackling with necromantic power, but my magic was back. I was able to call up a portal leading to the surface and carry you through it. The cat-sidhe was waiting, and brought us back here via a second portal."

"I thought I was hallucinating," Len said hoarsely.

Albigard eased back, his brow furrowing in concern. "So I gathered."

"Tell us everything you can remember, human," the cat-sidhe ordered. They still held the cup of steaming tea, and had not risen during Len's brief breakdown. But their green eyes were intent now, demanding answers.

Len sank down to sit on the pallet, feeling unaccountably relieved when Albigard joined him, perching primly on the edge of the bedding, shoulder to shoulder. He took a deep breath, trying to gather his thoughts into some kind of coherent narrative.

"When we first went into the tunnel, a lot of the roots seemed to be damaged," he began. "But others were only dormant, I guess. Albigard touched one of them and it whipped out and caught him by the wrist..."

He recounted the way the roots had trapped the Fae and used him to lure the Wild Hunt within reach... the way the Hunt had nearly escaped, and Len had collapsed the tunnel to trap it without truly understanding how he'd done it.

He described watching as the Hunt's darkness was pulled through the roots and siphoned into the body of the tree. Then, the reverse — something bright and golden traveling from inside the tree and into Albigard's body. He tried to put his confused flashes of consciousness into words — Albigard's heart bursting back into life beneath his ear, the gasp of breath as he'd regained awareness.

As Len finished speaking, something that had been circling at the edges of his thoughts for days now finally coalesced into solidity. He poked at it, trying to turn it around and see all the angles,

wondering if it could really be that simple—
because if so, the Fae Court had a hell of a lot to
answer for.

The cat-sidhe gave Albigard a contemplative
look. "Well, then, Albigard of the Unseelie. It appears that Mother Dhuinne has more use for you in
the realm of the living than the dead."

At Len's side, Albigard appeared faintly dazed
by both the retelling, and the sidhe's declaration.

"You believe my soul—and my magic—were
returned to my body by the world tree... with conscious intent?" he asked cautiously.

The cat-sidhe shrugged. "You both seem to
agree that the Hunt killed you, and there is little
question that Chaima absorbed the Hunt immediately afterward. I see no other explanation."

"Albigard thought Nigellus might be able to
use the Hunt as a conduit to reach Rans and
Zorah's souls," Len reminded the sidhe, trying to
follow the logic to its conclusion. "Maybe Chaima
did something similar? Or Dhuinne did, I guess,
because they seem to be the same thing."

"Your reasoning is sound," said the sidhe.
"The next step will be to see what sort of effect the
Hunt's absorption has had on Dhuinne's magical
imbalance. One assumes it can only be a positive
development, but it still does not address the underlying cause. That part remains a mystery."

Len took a deep, steadying breath, and spoke.
"No it doesn't. After seeing what I saw in that cavern, I think I know *exactly* what's causing the
problem."

FOURTEEN

Two sets of matching green eyes fell on Len with the weight of utter disbelief. He tried not to take it personally, since apparently no one on Dhuinne had managed to figure out the answer to the mystery in more than two hundred years of trying.

"It's the Unseelie," he said. "The roots of Chaima are sick, and the roots are elemental magic. Unseelie magic. But you've been sending the Unseelie to Earth for hundreds of years—sending them as changelings, ever since you won the war against the demons."

The cat-sidhe's lips parted. Albigard looked blank with shock.

"Don't you see?" Len asked. "At this point, there's probably more Unseelie magic on Earth than there is on Dhuinne. And the Hunt is basically Unseelie magic on steroids, right? It must have been attracted to Earth for ages now—like to like. So when the Court told it to hunt Albigard, and Albigard was on Earth, of course it broke through the veil to go after him."

His audience of two continued to stare at him with matching gobsmacked expressions. He cleared his throat, starting to feel more than a little self-conscious under the scrutiny.

"I think I first realized it properly when Chaima's roots went for Albigard like a cat going after a mouse, but they ignored me completely," he said. "I was too out of it at the time to really put it together, but it was as though they were ravenous for Unseelie energy. Albigard's. The Wild Hunt's. Maybe they couldn't suck anything out of Albigard because his magic was already gone, but they still sensed what he was. The roots are growing too weak to support the tree—that's why it's tilting. If it goes on for too long, it'll fall... and I'm guessing that would be bad with a capital B."

The cat-sidhe was still gaping at him. When he stopped speaking, the little Fae closed their mouth very deliberately and locked eyes with Albigard. "I will never question the perspicacity or intelligence of humans again," they said.

"I may," Albigard replied. "But when I do, you are welcome to remind me of this moment."

"So, I'm right?" Len pressed. "Because, to be fair I'm pulling this theory straight out of my ass. But it's the only thing I can see that fits all the facts."

"As you say, human," the cat-sidhe agreed. "I cannot refute the logic."

Albigard still looked decidedly dazed. "*Mab's green garden*. There are easily ten thousand Unseelie on Earth at present. Trying to recall all of them..."

It was Len's turn to be taken aback. "Ten... thousand? *Changelings*? As in, your people have kidnapped *ten thousand* human babies from Earth?"

He shook his head. "No, not changelings. Not all of them. That practice began as a way to subvert a particular treaty provision with the demons. Hell had negotiated a tithe from the Fae in exchange for peace—one-tenth of the children on Dhuinne were to be sent to them. That, along with Ransley Thorpe's survival, was the major concession we made in order to end the war quickly, after the rest of the vampires were killed."

"The demons neglected to specify that the children in question be Fae," the cat-sidhe added. "An omission I have always found interesting. Of course, the Court immediately sidestepped the provision by bringing human infants to Dhuinne, and sending them to Hell in place of our own children."

Albigard took up the thread again. "Fae are long-lived, and there are relatively few births—fewer than ever in recent years, perhaps due to the very same imbalance of magic we're currently discussing. Whatever the case, I would estimate that fewer than one thousand of the Unseelie on Earth are changelings. The rest are like me, sent to Earth because they were needed as additional support for the Fae power structure within the human realm."

Len knew he was still reeling from the previous day's events. He didn't really have the excess brainpower to devote to details, so he focused on the bottom line. "It doesn't matter. The Court needs to call them back to Dhuinne, or things are only going to get worse."

Utter silence greeted the words, as the other two exchanged glances.

"What?" Len demanded.

"Let us say that there is likely to be considerable resistance to that conclusion," the cat-sidhe replied.

Len stared at them. "So... what are you saying? The Court is just going to shrug and play the fiddle while Rome burns?"

The sidhe frowned. "I do not understand the reference."

Albigard sighed. "The Court would consider abdicating control of the Earth to be essentially the same as capitulating to the demons. There is also some question as to whether human institutions could survive the sudden removal of their hidden power structure."

"And if the world tree falls while the Fae are dicking around?" Len asked pointedly.

"There is a faction among the ruling class that was ready to abandon Dhuinne altogether and move the seat of power to Earth," Albigard reminded him.

"Which part of the last few weeks suggests that the devastation is going to be confined to a single realm?" Len demanded in exasperation.

"An excellent question," the cat-sidhe said grimly. "One which I would very much like to place before the Court for consideration."

"Yes." Albigard agreed. "Except for one small matter. In case you've forgotten, the leader of the Unseelie Court has already shown a willingness to sentence me to death, and to collar you with iron."

A look of stubbornness crossed the cat-sidhe's elfin features. "So he did. Yet here we both stand."

Len thought about the twins, Nezri and Da-non. "You know, you've got access to a—" He almost said 'a weapon,' but caught himself in time. "To allies that you're not using."

A furrow formed between Albigard's brows. "The Forsaken? I'm not certain they will have much interest in confronting the same government that forced them into exile in the first place."

But Len didn't back down. "What makes you so sure? They already have spies in the city. And they've risked themselves to help us trap the Hunt."

"Perhaps," said the cat-sidhe, in a tone of speculation.

"Can we find them and ask?" Len replied. "It might be several days until they come back here."

"It's not an unreasonable course of action, I suppose," Albigard allowed. "For one thing, we will need food, and the area around the camp has been severely impacted by the Hunt's passage."

Len hadn't been outside the cave yet. His heart sank at the idea that they might have caused the camp's destruction. "Did it kill everything?"

But Albigard shook his head. "The damage isn't comparable to the damage you saw on Earth, or in the pocket realm. Many plants and animals were killed, it is true. Others were weakened. But this is Dhuinne. Life will recover quickly."

That was both a relief, and an unwelcome reminder of what might have happened back on Earth in Len's absence. At the moment, however, there wasn't much he could do about Earth. It was safe from additional attacks, now that the Wild

Hunt had been absorbed into the world tree, but he had no way to find out what damage had already been done.

The cat-sidhe tilted their head at Albigard. "There is a faint connection through you, leading to the twins."

He nodded. "They were able to track you by following the thread you left when you gifted me your magic in California. No doubt you are feeling that same connection, from the other end."

"That would explain it, yes." The sidhe stood up and dusted off their buckskin breeches. "It should not be difficult to trace them."

Still seated next to Len on the edge of the pallet, Albigard turned and gave him an assessing look. "Are you recovered enough to travel?"

In truth, Len felt like he could sleep for a solid week. But... it was pretty clear they weren't done yet.

"Take me someplace with food, and I'll manage," he said. "Just don't expect me to battle any more deadly Fae archetypes for a bit, okay?"

"Don't even *think* such a thing," Albigard replied, looking appalled. "What was that you mentioned earlier, about tempting fate?"

Len hid the stupid, sappy grin that wanted to escape in response to the jab... because Albigard was *alive*. Somehow, against all good sense, the Fae was still here—and just for this one moment, Len could ignore all the other calamities hanging over their heads on the strength of that one impossible, amazing fact.

As the cat-sidhe had promised, finding the temporary Forsaken camp wasn't difficult. Apparently the group hadn't gone far—not that it really mattered, when getting back to them was a simple matter of stepping through the cat-sidhe's portal.

There was a bit of a tense standoff when they arrived, with surprised Forsaken lunging for weapons and calling magic to hand. It was pretty clear they hadn't expected the cat-sidhe to return from Chaima so quickly... or for Albigard to return at all. Fortunately, recognition rippled through the camp before anyone started hurling either arrows or blasts of power at them. Nezri hurried forward, Danon only a few steps behind her.

"What happened?" she demanded. "Were you unable to..." She trailed off, her eyes falling heavily on Albigard. "Wait. Your magic is back. How—?"

Danon joined his sister and gave the three of them a piercing, head-to-toe sweep. "Maybe you should come to the fire and sit down for a bit. You look like you could use some food and a hot drink before you tell us what happened."

"Yes, please," Len managed weakly, only to stifle a groan when he remembered that he shouldn't accept food and drink from Fae.

Albigard must have intuited his problem, because he cupped a hand beneath Len's elbow and shepherded him in the direction the twins indicated, murmuring, "You need not fear. The bond between us returned at the same time as my magic.

You are still claimed, and may not be claimed by another."

Intellectually, Len knew that shouldn't have been a relief... and yet, he was relieved. It *definitely* shouldn't have sent a low curl of heat through his belly. He let out a slow breath and rummaged in his pocket with his free hand, pulling out the battered hair tie and showing it to his companion.

"Guess I should have ditched this old thing when I had the chance, huh?" he quipped.

Albigard raised a wry eyebrow. "As I have explained before, it doesn't work like that. But, as I have more use for such an item than you..."

He lifted a hand as though to reach for the strip of cloth.

"Nope, get your own." Len snatched it away and put it back in his pocket. "Taking gifts back is tacky."

He was certain he could sense Albigard's aura of smug satisfaction radiating against his left side like sunlight. The contented feeling kindling in Len's chest in response was unexpected, but maybe it shouldn't have been. Reassured on a number of different levels, he accepted a place near the campfire and a bowl of some kind of hearty soup, which he ate ravenously.

Len had always possessed an affinity for food and its preparation, but the last few weeks had honed his appreciation of nourishment to a sharp edge. When he'd been homeless, he'd missed plenty of meals. He'd gone hungry sometimes, but he'd never thought about *real starvation*... about having no access to food for days or weeks on end, and knowing that the lack of it might well end up causing his death.

Since the pocket realm, every meal had tasted like life; like the promise of another day. And all that was *before* you factored in the savory addictiveness of even the simplest Faerie food.

With his hunger and thirst sated, Len sat with Albigard at his side and let the cat-sidhe take the lead in explaining what had happened over the course of the last day. When the sidhe reached the part about the Unseelie migration to Earth causing the imbalance in Dhuinne's magic, Nezri's eyebrows shot up.

"What made you realize, Elder?" she asked, looking every bit as taken aback as Albigard and the cat-sidhe had, when Len first dumped the idea on them.

"I did not realize," said the elfin Fae. "It was the human who solved the mystery."

Abruptly, all eyes turned to Len, who shifted in place with an awkward cough.

"It was the roots, beneath Chaima," he told the small crowd. "You said they represented Unseelie magic, and they've been weakened. The way I understand it, that means Unseelie magic on Dhuinne has also been weakened... which makes sense, since a bunch of the Unseelie Fae aren't here anymore."

"It makes a certain amount of sense, when you frame it like that," Danon said. "So, what can we do to fix it?"

The cat-sidhe wore a grim, contemplative expression. "That is the question, is it not?"

Albigard steepled his fingers beneath his chin. "The Court will not look kindly on any demand to recall the Unseelie from the human realm," he said. "Yet they are the only ones with the power to do so. I believe we must confront them with the truth, regardless of the consequences."

Nezri tilted her head. "Dhuinne restored your life after you sacrificed it in her service. That is no small thing to be dismissed out of hand — not even by the Court."

The old woman, Aesulna, had been watching the proceedings closely. "Perhaps. But do not forget, members of the Court also laid hands on a sidhe. The old ways are crumbling. Still, there must be some in the city who will see sense."

"If we all go together, we might get their attention," Danon said. Then he shrugged. "Or they might attack us on sight. Hard to say which."

"With the Hunt neutralized, we have time now, at least," the cat-sidhe declared. "First, we will rest. The Unseelie and his human were both hard-used in the caverns beneath Chaima. They need time to recover. Decisions about our approach to the Court can wait until tomorrow, at the earliest."

Nezri nodded. "If the Hunt is no longer a danger, we could return to the camp today... though it would require some organization. This place isn't nearly as well defended."

"It might be best to wait a few days, until the area recovers," said the cat-sidhe. "The devastation was extensive, and food in the valley is scarce. Did you bring your stores with you?"

"We did," said Aesulna. "We'll be fine here for a bit."

After a bit more discussion, the meeting broke up into smaller groups. Many people left to resume whatever tasks they'd been doing when Len, Albigard, and the cat-sidhe had portaled in. The sidhe wandered away with Nezri and Aesulna, the three of them deep in conversation.

Danon gave Len and Albigard an assessing glance. "Get some rest," he ordered gruffly, and tossed a pile of blankets and furs at their feet before leaving as well.

Len let out a sigh like a deflating balloon in response to the idea that they might finally have a day to just... *be*. No Wild Hunt breathing down their necks. No jail cells. No expectation of certain death looming around the corner—though Len still couldn't quite credit how things had turned out on that particular front.

Movement caught his eye, and he looked up to find Leesa approaching them. Her face was alight with happiness.

"You're all right!" she exclaimed, by way of a greeting, and flopped down to sit cross-legged in front of them.

Len wasn't sure he was ever going to be 'all right' again, but he appreciated the sentiment.

"The outcome was unexpected, to put it mildly," Albigard replied, in the understatement of the decade.

"It turns out, he's so prickly that even Chaima spat him out," Len managed.

The grin that split Leesa's face was like a flash of blue sky after a cloudy day. "I'm *so* glad. For both of you."

"Me, too," Len said, and felt everything unexpectedly hit him again.

"Can you tell me about Chaima?" Leesa asked brightly. "I've never talked to anyone who's really been there. What are the magical fields like around it?"

Albigard must have noticed the slump of Len's shoulders as the last of his energy deserted him, because he said, "A moment, first. Then I would be happy to discuss it with you." He shook out the pile of blankets Danon had left them and laid them on the ground. When he was done, he turned to Len. "Sleep now. You are not yet recovered from your ordeal."

"What about *your* ordeal?" Len prodded.

The Fae's expression softened. "I am well. Or at least, I believe I would prefer a pleasant conversation regarding magical theory to additional rest at the moment. *I* was not the one who collapsed a tunnel entrance using untried powers of necromancy, after all."

No, Len thought. *You were the one who died.*

"Okay," he said aloud. "Try not to corrupt her too badly while I'm napping."

Leesa scoffed at his words.

Len reminded himself one more time that things were fine now, for a given definition — albeit one that didn't extend to the mess they'd left behind on Earth. He'd be obsessing over that part soon enough, but Albigard was right. First, he needed to sleep. He made himself comfortable on the nest of blankets Albigard had prepared for him and closed his eyes, letting the others' incomprehensible discussion about recursive dimensional folds and diffuse semi-permeable tesseract barriers lull his mind into silence.

FIFTEEN

Len jerked awake repeatedly throughout the day, tormented by dreams in which Albigard died again and again as Len kissed him, and the Hunt escaped to wreak more havoc across the realms.

Each time, strong hands steadied him, a familiar voice murmuring words of reassurance and urging him back to sleep. Len tried to feel guilt over the realization that Albigard was apparently stuck at his bedside, playing nursemaid — and couldn't.

Eventually, Leesa woke him to give him more soup. Evening was giving way to night, and Albigard was still there, sipping his own bowl without offering any comment regarding Len's shiny new parasomnia disorder.

"Is everything still all right?" Len muttered around mouthfuls of soup.

"All is well," Albigard assured him.

Len finished the bowl and put it down. "All might be well *here*," he said, unable to set aside his other worries any longer. "But what about on Earth? And if the Hunt is gone, that means Rans and Zorah—"

"Yes," Albigard said dully, cutting him off. "It does seem likely that they are truly lost."

The Fae rose and walked out of the circle of firelight, his movements abrupt and jerky. Len closed his eyes and let him have the moment alone. He got up more slowly, and took the opportunity to find a convenient tree at the edge of the camp to piss on. When he was done, he prodded at the ugly dark hole where all his worries about his friends on Earth lived.

When it came to Rans and Zorah being dead, nothing had changed — not really. They'd been dead before, with only a single, crazy long shot at getting them back. They were still dead. The fact that the long shot now looked to be completely impossible shouldn't have mattered to his grief.

Somehow, it still did.

He returned to the pile of blankets to find Albigard waiting for him, contemplating the fire. Around them, the other members of the camp were settling in for the night. Len joined him, watching the hypnotic flicker of the flames.

"I'm sorry," he said, his gaze sliding sideways to rest on his companion's somber features. "I miss them, too."

Albigard nodded, his eyes bright in the firelight, and did not resist as Len pulled him to lie down on the nest of blankets. The Fae's arm came around Len's torso from behind, and Albigard rested his forehead against the nape of Len's neck. With their bodies pressed together and the reassurance of Albigard's heartbeat thudding strong and steady against Len's back, the nightmares didn't wake him again.

As it turned out, Len didn't need nightmares to pull him out of a sound sleep. The cries of, '*Wake up, something's breaching the wards!*' were highly effective in achieving the same result.

Albigard cursed in that unfamiliar language he sometimes used, rolling smoothly to his feet while Len was still flailing clumsily out of the blankets. By the time Len got himself upright and blinked his eyes into focus in the gray light of predawn, his companion's clothing had melted into the magic-infused, dark leather battle armor he'd worn in St. Louis.

"Stay low," Albigard hissed. "I don't know where the threat is coming from yet."

Len dropped back to a crouch, painfully aware that he'd be useless in any kind of a magical battle. Around them, the Forsaken were scrambling for weapons. There was a sharp whistle, and someone was tossing Albigard a sword, hilt-first. One of the other camp members made a quick gesture toward the fire, and it extinguished as though it had never been — snuffed out without a single ember or wisp of smoke.

"The kids," Len said, low and urgent. "There are *children* here, for god's sake—"

Albigard paced in a wary circle around him, his attention focused outward. "We must trust that the Forsaken have a plan for their own defense," he said grimly.

And before Len could answer, dark shapes swarmed the camp from all directions. The Forsaken roared a ragged battle cry, and magic started flying. Len did as he'd been told and stayed on the ground, hunched low as blasts of light illuminated the clearing with a crazy strobe effect.

The attackers were Fae—Seelie and Unseelie—dressed in uniforms similar to the guards who'd escorted Len and Albigard to and from the Court a few days ago. They were armed with blades as well as magic, and Len scrambled out of the way as one of the intruders, a Seelie warrior, clashed with Albigard in a flurry of sword strikes.

He only just managed to brace himself for the blast of icy power when the woman screamed and fell, pierced through the heart. Albigard hoisted Len up by one arm while he was still trying to force oxygen into frozen lungs.

"There are too many," Albigard grated out. "We will make for better cover."

Len stumbled after the Fae as he headed toward the denser forest surrounding the camp, sword held ready in his other hand. Behind them, Len could hear screams and curses.

"The others!" he gasped, trying to turn back.

Albigard didn't slow, or let go of his grip on Len's arm. "You are unarmed and human, not to mention under my protection, now that I am in any position to offer such a thing. Your safety takes precedence—"

Of course, that was the moment three Fae warriors descended on them. Albigard snarled and shoved Len backward. His hand lifted, fingers curling like an orchestra conductor, and one of the attackers yelped as the ever-present vines surrounding them tangled around his ankles. Another one hurled a ball of crackling flames at Albigard's face. He lifted his sword faster than Len's eyes could follow. The magical attack crackled against the iron blade and dispersed.

The two who were still free descended on Albigard with weapons clashing and whirling, tag-teaming him. Meanwhile, the third assailant was struggling to free his limbs from the entangling vines, which had his sword-arm wrapped up now, as well.

Fae are tough, Rans had said. *Not much can kill them permanently except iron through the heart. Or, well, beheading.*

Len waited until the vicious battle moved a few yards away and darted in, putting his full weight behind a vicious roundhouse right to the trapped Fae's jaw. When the man sagged, disoriented, he yanked the sword from his vine-wrapped grip and slammed the hilt into the Fae's temple, felling him. He crashed to the ground and lay still.

Since Len had no idea how to use the thing for either defense or offense, he hurled the blade into the impenetrable brush nearby, where it at least wouldn't end up in one of their attacker's hands. While he was confident that he hadn't accidentally killed his victim by bashing him in the side of the head, he hoped like hell that Fae healing ability also meant he hadn't just caused the man a permanent brain injury.

It was clear Albigard did not share Len's qualms when it came to the invaders' ultimate wellbeing. Blood spurted from the neck of one of his opponents, and the man fell with a horrible gurgling sound. Len tried to brace for it, but no fresh blast of death energy hit him this time.

Apparently, a sliced throat did not equal beheading.

The remaining invader ducked under Albigard's guard, and Len heard his companion grunt as the Seelie's flashing blade caught him across the thigh. Albigard used the momentum of his stumble to slam into her with his full weight. They went down in a tangle. Magic flared between them like crackling electricity, and when Albigard rolled away with a groan, the Seelie lay unmoving on the ground.

Len hurried to Albigard's side and grabbed him by the wrist, hauling him upright. Albigard staggered to his feet, sword still in hand. Behind them, shouts and running footsteps warned that the skirmish hadn't gone unnoticed by the rest of the attacking forces.

"Can you walk?" Len asked tightly, reminding himself firmly that the Fae had walked away from a spectacular car crash in a vehicle with no airbags or modern crumple zones. A sword slash across the thigh was nothing.

"Yes, I—" Albigard breathed in sharply, cutting himself off, and whirled to face in the other direction.

Len whipped his head around, fully expecting to see more armed Fae swarming toward them from the direction of the trees. Instead, his stomach twisted with queasiness, as clammy sweat broke out across his skin.

"No," he breathed, recognizing the unmistakable sensation for exactly what it was. Sick denial drained the blood from his face, as rolling, greasy black smoke emerged from the dense tangle of woods. "*No!*"

Albigard stared at the oily vapor as though mesmerized, heedless of the half-dozen attackers bearing down on them from the other direction. With a wordless, animal noise, Len slammed into the Fae's body and bore him to the ground, caging him beneath arms and legs as a litany of *no, no, no, it's not fair, this can't be happening* echoed through his mind.

Choking black smoke poured over them. Len's heart pounded against his ribs like a wild animal trying to escape a cage.

"*You can't have him!*" he snarled — irrationally, as though the Wild *fucking* Hunt cared one whit about Len's words.

He clung to Albigard's prone body for endless moments until the Hunt flowed away, leaving clear air and the first hint of dawn lighting the forest. Terrified of what he would find, Len tried to detect any hint of movement or life beneath him, past his own thundering heartbeat and heaving chest.

"Don't be dead," he begged. "Please, not again, not *again* —"

A hand closed around his upper arm, clad in a creaking leather gauntlet. Len gasped, nearly choking on it.

Albigard eased him back, and Len swallowed a noise that might have been a sob.

"I am well," said the Fae, his bloodless complexion belying the words somewhat. As though aware of how that sounded, he added, "For a given definition, at any rate. Let me up."

Len wasn't entirely sure his legs were going to follow his instructions to that degree, but he managed to roll off Albigard's body and make it to a kneeling position in the thick grass. His head swam, but his eyes fell on a pile of dark shapes about a dozen yards away. Farther away, the shouts and curses of battle from the main camp had turned into screams of terror. Len's stomach heaved.

The pair of them managed to get to their feet, leaning on each other heavily. "Should we try to run?" Len asked, well aware that his brain was too muddled for reasonable decision-making.

Albigard paused. "If it were after me, it would not have moved away while I still lived. And running from the Hunt has never served us well."

Len nodded, dry-mouthed. They stumbled toward the camp, half holding each other up. The Fae warriors who had been charging toward them lay twisted on the ground, wearing the familiar expressions of fixed horror that Len had already seen far too many times on victims of the Hunt.

As they reached the site of the main battle, the sun breached the treetops, spilling light over a scene that stole Len's breath.

Dead attackers lay on the ground where they had fallen, while the Forsaken stood by with weapons hanging lax from their hands. All of them were turned in one direction, eyes fixed on the quiescent pall of oily black smoke that hung there. It lay draped across the landscape on the far side of the camp, floating motionless and unthreatening in the early morning illumination.

SIXTEEN

"What... the hell... is *happening*?" Len asked blankly, staring at the unlikely tableau. He ignored the brief look of irritation Albigard shot him, presumably in response to the invocation of the demon realm.

They continued closer. A few of the bodies lying on the ground were, in fact, Forsaken — but they were burned or bloody, victims of the battle rather than the Hunt, Len would have bet. His eyes fell on movement as the cat-sidhe rose from examining one of the dead Fae invaders. The shape-shifter's green gaze flickered over Len and Albigard as they approached, acknowledging their survival with a short, satisfied nod.

No one answered Len's rather plaintive question, probably because no one else had a clue what was going on either.

"Perhaps I will ask the Hunt to explain," said the sidhe.

There was an audible intake of breath as the shape-shifter turned and walked directly toward the dark mass. Len twitched toward them, but Albigard's hand closed around his forearm, aborting the movement.

"Let the sidhe do as they wish," he murmured, a look of speculation settling over his pale features.

Len chewed at his lip ring as the sidhe strode up to the edge of the Hunt's darkness and paused. The shape-shifter lifted one hand, and a tentative curl of black smoke reached out to coil around it. Breath caught in Len's chest.

The sidhe stood motionless for what felt like several minutes. Albigard maintained his grip on Len's arm, his tension clear in the grasp of his fingers.

Eventually, the Hunt's vaporous appendage retracted into the main mass of the cloud. The cat-sidhe stared at the deadly Fae monster, head tilted in silent contemplation. One of the Forsaken stepped forward, and Len recognized Nezri. Danon joined her, his broad chest dripping red from an ugly slash across his left pectoral muscle.

"Well?" Nezri demanded, voicing the question echoing in everyone's thoughts.

The sidhe let out a long breath and turned their back on the Hunt to address the survivors.

"The Wild Hunt no longer serves the Fae Court," they said, without preamble.

Silence fell around the clearing. After a long moment, Albigard broke it.

"Then who... or what... *does* it serve?"

"It serves Dhuinne."

Len blinked.

"As in... it serves the Fae realm directly?" he asked, tentative.

"Indeed," the cat-sidhe said. "It now acts in the best interest of Dhuinne, whatever that may entail."

Danon shifted warily. "And how are we supposed to know what it thinks is in Dhuinne's best interest?"

The cat-sidhe met Len and Albigard's eyes in turn. One dark eyebrow arched. "I daresay we will have to use our best judgment."

Albigard's grip tightened on Len's arm for a second, and then he very deliberately let go. "We must go to the Court," he said. "*Today*."

"That's suicide," Danon said.

Albigard flicked an abbreviated gesture at the carnage in the camp... at the Hunt. "Is it really, though?" he asked.

Nezri crossed her arms, frowning. "There's no reason to assume that just because it killed these guards, it's going to follow you to the Court like your tame guard dog."

The sidhe tapped a finger to their lip, thoughtful. "And yet... our intention is to demand the recall of the Unseelie from Earth, in order to heal the imbalance in Dhuinne's magic. Is there anything more directly relevant to Dhuinne's survival at present?"

Nezri drew breath to speak, only to hesitate.

"Did any of the attacking forces escape?" Albigard asked.

Danon answered. "Some of them portaled away to safety when they saw what was happening."

Len followed that train of thought to its likely conclusion. "So, it's a pretty good guess they ran straight back to the Court to report on what happened, right?"

"To the Court... or perhaps to Oren," Albigard replied grimly.

Len snorted. "I bet they'll start taking the Hunt seriously *now*," he muttered. Then he glanced around the camp, and a sudden jolt of worry hit him. "Hang on — the children. Where are they?"

But Nezri turned and addressed the sidhe. "Do you deem it safe now, Elder?"

The cat-sidhe nodded. "I do."

Nezri and Danon locked eyes, and Nezri spoke words Len didn't understand. A vortex of air in an open area near the center of the camp shimmered like heat haze in the morning sun, before seeming to collapse on itself. Inside, the children huddled, unharmed. Len let out a heartfelt sigh of relief.

Leesa had a toddler resting on her hip, with an older boy's hand held in hers. She looked around with wide eyes that grew even wider when they landed on the Wild Hunt. Several adults hurried forward to sweep the children up and take them away, murmuring comfort and explanations.

Others began seeing to the wounded, though Danon waved away Aesulna's attempt to look at the slice across his chest. Len counted three figures wearing the ragged clothing of the Forsaken among the dead scattered on the ground. Several people clustered around them. Some were weeping.

As much as it sickened him, given the scale of the attack, Len knew it could have been much worse.

"I will travel to the city, once all of the wounded have been seen to," Albigard declared evenly. His eyes sought out the cat-sidhe's. "Will you accompany me, Elder?"

"Of course I will, *a leanbh*," said the shape-shifter. "Was there ever any doubt?"

Albigard's gaze slid to Len, an unspoken question.

"Wouldn't miss it," he said ironically, because if Albigard thought Len was letting him out of his sight anytime in the next century, he was smoking crack.

Nezri and Danon exchanged looks.

"If you are confronting the Court, you will need a show of power," Nezri said. "As much as you can muster. We will accompany you as well, along with anyone else from the camp who cares to lend their strength to the cause of saving Dhuinne from its own leaders."

"Count me in," Aesulna said tartly, looking up from the injured Fae she was hovering over.

"Do we have any sort of strategy beyond marching up to the Court and demanding they listen to us?" Len asked. "Because no offense, but that seems a bit... vague?"

Albigard quirked an eyebrow. "If the Wild Hunt deigns to accompany us, I doubt any additional strategy will be required."

Len asked the obvious follow-up question. "And if it doesn't?"

The Fae's expression turned wry. "Then I don't believe additional strategy will help."

"Right." Len blew out a breath and gave him a pointed onceover. "How about we at least hold off until you look less like you're about to fall over."

He hesitated. "And until I *feel* less like I'm about to fall over."

Aesulna snorted.

"I did say, 'once all the wounded have been seen to,'" Albigard pointed out mildly.

"So you did," Len replied. He turned to survey the scene. "Let's get on with that, shall we?"

———————◆———————

It was the ass-end of mid-morning before the camp members finished dealing with all the dead bodies, in addition to the living ones. The more superficial wounds like the slice on Albigard's thigh and the gash on Danon's chest were largely healed, thanks to a combination of magical medicine and innate Fae toughness. The more serious injuries were at least stabilized, and would heal soon enough.

Len reflected — not for the first time in recent days — that sleeping for a week solid sounded an awful lot like heaven. Unfortunately, that wasn't in the cards. Though he did feel like imminent collapse was no longer a concern, thankfully. The shock of thinking he'd lost Albigard to the Hunt for a second time had faded a bit, and the icy blast of fresh Fae death animus had settled into place.

Even so, after so long spent with his old, familiar collection of specters, he was finding this current revolving door of necromantic energy... *disconcerting*.

He knew nothing whatsoever about the dead Seelie warrior whose animus now swirled around him like a chilly cloud, beyond the fact that she'd been enthusiastically attempting to kill Albigard when he'd succeeded in killing her instead. The Unseelie attacker Len had knocked out with the hilt of his own sword had only died later, when the Hunt rolled over him.

At some point, Len would have to decide what he felt about that, if anything.

None of the invading Fae who'd remained behind had survived. No one was quite sure how many had portaled away to safety — only that some of them had. Albigard seemed to think that would work in their favor. Len had pretty much given up on the whole *optimism* gig these days, but nevertheless hoped he was right about that.

The big question remained — would the Hunt tag along with them when they traveled to the city to confront the Court, or wander off and leave them to their own devices? So far, it had shown no inclination to leave. It was still hovering in exactly the same place where it had come to rest after the battle.

When Nezri and Aesulna proclaimed the members of the camp as ready as they could be, the cat-sidhe approached the edge of the sinuous black cloud and extended a hand. As before, the Hunt reciprocated, reaching out to touch. Len didn't panic this time, but his nerves still thrummed with misgivings.

Albigard joined him, standing next to his shoulder.

"Do you think they can actually communicate like that?" Len asked. The cat-sidhe certainly seemed to think so, but Len was still struggling with the idea of a terrifying cloud of death and awfulness being sentient in the first place.

Albigard shrugged, his leather armor creaking with the small movement. "Both the sidhe and the Wild Hunt are ancient aspects of Dhuinne."

Len shot him a sidelong glance. "I can't help noticing, you're staking an awful lot on the idea that the Hunt's on our side now."

"Yes," Albigard agreed simply.

The cat-sidhe pulled back, and the Hunt did the same.

"It is time to proceed," said the shape-shifter. "Let all who intend to join us stand ready."

Perhaps two-dozen Forsaken took up arms and fell into ragged formation behind Len and Albigard. The Hunt twisted restlessly as the sidhe joined the group.

"Where will you transport us?" Nezri asked. "The portal zone behind the Court building?"

The cat-sidhe let out a little huff. "Hardly. We will enter the chamber itself. One does like to make an emphatic statement in situations such as this."

Albigard frowned. "The Court's meeting gallery is heavily protected. Can you do that?"

The cat-sidhe gave him a patient look. "What have I told you about wards crafted by Seelie and Unseelie, youngling?"

With that, the shape-shifter lifted one delicate hand and made an intricate gesture with curled fingers. Len squared his shoulders as a portal large enough for three people to enter abreast burned itself into the air. Albigard exchanged a glance with him, and they strode through in the cat-sidhe's wake.

SEVENTEEN

L en forced himself not to sway or stumble as the familiar sense of disorientation hit him, and then he was in the Court chamber with its thick moss and overgrown, flowering vines covering the walls and benches.

Chaos erupted as spectators and members of the Court surged to their feet. The first cry of, *'Guards!'* was quickly echoed by others, as the Forsaken marched through the portal after the cat-sidhe, Albigard, and Len. Scanning the echoing space with a quick sweep of his eyes, Len got the impression that they'd barged in on some kind of high-level meeting. A good twenty or more Unseelie in their glittering finery occupied the space beneath the dais, where Len and Albigard had stood like criminals on trial not so long ago. All of them had whirled in surprise at the appearance of the portal, but they weren't running away as many of the spectators had done.

Len's attention caught on a familiar head of copper-blonde hair topping a haughty, sharp-featured face.

Teague.

What the hell was Albigard's wayward protégé doing here, when he should be on Earth?

He couldn't worry about it now, though — not with guards charging toward them from all directions. A translucent barrier whirled into existence around their group just as the first blast of magic flew at them. It exploded against the shimmering shield, and Len chanced a glance over his shoulder to see Nezri and Danon with their hands raised in a strong blocking gesture.

The cat-sidhe strode forward as more blasts slammed against the twins' protection, slipping through the shield as though it didn't exist and swiping aside a stray blast from the guards with a sharp gesture of one hand.

"Do. *Not*." The sidhe snarled, sounding every bit the part of an angry cat.

The female Magistrate who'd questioned Albigard and Len during their last visit to this room stood warily as the cat-sidhe approached the dais. She raised a quelling hand as some of the Unseelie gathered in front of the Court made as though to attack, and addressed the sidhe directly.

"What is the meaning of this?" she demanded, imperious and cool despite the sudden appearance of an armed contingent inside her domain.

Len glanced behind him again, thinking that this would be a really good time for the Hunt to make an appearance through the portal that was still flaming away in the middle of the aisle. There was no sign of the damned thing.

The cat-sidhe marched through the mass of gathered Unseelie. They melted aside with clear reluctance — making just enough room for the little shape-shifter to pass by without bumping shoulders. The sidhe didn't stop, climbing the steps onto the dais without hesitation.

Len scanned the raised platform for Oren, and found him in his customary place at the center of the Unseelie Court. He was on his feet like most of the others, his shoulders tight with tension and his expression rigid.

"Stop this duplicitous creature!" he barked.

The sidhe didn't back down. "You already tried that once, Oren of the Unseelie," they said, in a tone dripping ice. "I would urge you *not* to try it again."

Oren sputtered. The cat-sidhe ignored him and walked straight up to the Magistrate's desk.

"Explain yourself, Elder," the Magistrate demanded.

"You've traitors inside your nest, Magistrate," said the shape-shifter, lifting a hand toward Oren. "This Fae and his allies have conspired against the best interest of Mother Dhuinne. They have courted chaos in two realms... and, on a more personal note, they have laid hands on a sidhe."

Albigard stepped forward, though he was careful to stay inside the twins' protection. "Oren and his allies captured the cat-sidhe on Earth, and chained them in iron in a secret underground location outside the city," he said evenly, his voice cutting across the confusion in the room.

Oren straightened as though someone had shoved a ramrod up his spine. "Are we to listen to the ravings of this condemned criminal?" he demanded. "Or to a sidhe who conspires with demons? Call more guards—crush this rabble who would dare violate the Court chamber!"

The sidhe turned to him, the movement slow and dangerous as the guards arrayed around the room wavered, unsure whose orders they were supposed to be listening to.

"Do you deny the accusation?" asked the shape-shifter. "No Seelie or Unseelie may lay hands on a sidhe. I was here before your ancestors started banging rocks together to make tools, Oren of the Court. It is likely I will be here long after you are gone to dust. *Answer with care.*"

Len held his breath. Beside him, Albigard's spine was a solid line of tension.

Oren lifted his chin. "I have no need to answer one who gives aid and comfort to Dhuinne's enemies. The words of such a creature are not to be trusted."

The cat-sidhe reached into a pouch hanging from their belt and pulled out a tiny iron collar attached to a length of iron chain. They held it out mockingly for a long moment, and let it clatter onto the Magistrate's desk without a word.

Silence fell over the room, brittle as glass.

"This is a serious accusation," the Magistrate said slowly. "Yet it does not explain your unprecedented invasion of the inner Court chamber. You descend with armed barbarians and escaped criminals, rather than making your complaint through the proper channels."

"There is more you need to hear, Your Grace," Albigard said. "Despite the best attempts of this body to deny the scope of the problem and obstruct any viable solution, the Wild Hunt has been contained — reabsorbed into Dhuinne through the roots of Chaima, the world-tree. But much remains to be done before Dhuinne may once more be whole... and it will not be done as long as you have vipers hiding among you."

Oren's fingers were curled into claws on the polished wood of the desk in front of him. "The Hunt clearly is *not* under control, traitor... *since you still live.*"

Hatred for this man — who would see his own son dead for refusing to support his shortsighted and cruel actions — raised gooseflesh along Len's back. Or... maybe that feeling was caused by something else, since a wave of clammy queasiness washed over him a second later.

"You think it is not under control? I must beg to differ... *Father*," Albigard replied in a poisonous tone.

The Hunt poured through the portal, spilling into the chamber like ink poured into a glass of water.

The room erupted into screams. Roughly two-thirds of the people still present scrambled for the nearest exits, apparently unable to portal away with the Court's protective wards in place.

Len kept a tight grip on his own instinctive panic, which had only been mildly diminished by the Hunt's recent behavior and the cat-sidhe's reassurance about the Fae archetype's abrupt change of heart. It was just about all he could do not to tackle Albigard to the ground again, as the oily mass rolled past without touching them. If Albigard shared Len's lingering fear, the Fae hid it perfectly beneath a granite mask.

To their credit, none of the Court members joined the fleeing masses... nor did the group of Unseelie higher-ups who'd gathered to meet with them. It might have been courage. Or it might have had something to do with the fact that up until recently, the Court had called the shots regarding whom the Wild Hunt targeted.

"*Where is the cu-sidhe*?" Oren demanded, his voice gone high-pitched.

"Probably still in the crypt where you sent them," the cat-sidhe said, perfectly deadpan. "To guard *me*."

Len, who'd been keeping half an eye on Teague out of enlightened self-preservation, saw the backstabbing bastard send Albigard a wide-eyed look as the Hunt poured into the area where he and his fellow Unseelie were standing. It swirled over them and up the steps to the dais without slowing, obscuring the entire front of the chamber for long moments.

Albigard stood frozen next to Len, his fists clenched at his sides. It occurred to Len that no one was really sure what it meant—in real-world terms—that the Hunt was now serving Dhuinne. Had it just killed the entire Court, along with the gathered Unseelie higher-ups, effectively lopping the head off the Fae government as they stood by and watched?

Would it be a bad thing if it *had*?

After a seemingly endless stretch, that probably lasted less than twenty seconds in reality, the dark cloud ebbed like a wave retreating from the beach. The cat-sidhe stood, unmoved — still locking gazes with the Magistrate, who looked pale as a sheet... though undeniably alive.

The other members of the Seelie Court were also still standing. As were... some of the Unseelie Court members. Len heard the faint, punched-out noise that slipped past Albigard's control. An instant later, he identified one of the half-dozen or so figures slumped across the long wooden desk as Oren.

Dead at the hands of the same force he'd tried to unleash on his son.

The Hunt retreated from the area below the dais, revealing another four dead Unseelie lying sprawled on the moss-covered floor. Len was distantly surprised to see that Teague was not among them. Like the others who'd survived, Albigard's protégé looked dazed, as though he couldn't quite wrap his mind around what had just happened.

The cat-sidhe turned to survey the carnage, green eyes falling on Oren's collapsed body. "Well," they said in a philosophical tone, "I did warn him that I would outlive him."

Behind Len, one of the Forsaken let out an indelicate snort. Danon, maybe.

Len brushed fingers over the back of Albigard's hand, trusting that everyone else was too distracted to notice the small gesture. The Fae's skin was ice cold, and he gave a small flinch of surprise at the contact. In the next moment, Len felt as much as saw him draw that same ice around him like armor. Every hint of vulnerability fled, locked tight behind a glacial bearing and haughty demeanor that would have done Oren proud.

With a deep breath, Albigard straightened his shoulders and strode out of the protection of the twins' magical shield. Despite his misgivings, Len let him go, knowing that this was something he had to do alone. Dhuinne was not Len's world. It was Albigard's—and the Forsaken's, too—even if its leaders had tried to renounce them.

The twins' barrier spun itself out to nothing, no longer necessary with the Hunt swirling around their ragged group in clear and unmistakable warning. Dead silence fell over the echoing chamber, broken only by Albigard's boot heels as he strode up the stairs to the dais, his leather battle armor melting back into silk brocade and sleek black breeches as he ascended.

When he reached the Unseelie side of the Court, he came to a halt in front of Oren's corpse, collapsed across the polished wood of the long desk. After staring down at the unmoving body for a long moment, he placed a hand on its shoulder and shoved it away. It slid to the floor behind the desk and landed with a dull thump, out of sight.

Someone gasped.

Albigard turned to face the chamber and leaned his hips against the solid length of wood, supremely unconcerned by the presence of the surviving Unseelie Court members at his back. He looked across the divide at the Seelie, the picture of lethal elegance.

EIGHTEEN

The Magistrate met Albigard's gaze, lifting her chin as though steeling herself. "The Wild Hunt," she said. "Have you somehow taken control of it?"

"Hardly," he replied.

"And yet it does your bidding," the Magistrate shot back.

"Not *my* bidding," Albigard told her.

"Then whose?" she demanded.

"The Wild Hunt now serves Dhuinne," Albigard said. "And none other."

The Magistrate's eyes flew to the cat-sidhe, who shrugged.

"Why are you looking at me?" they asked. "Do you doubt his word?"

The Seelie leader's mouth opened, but no words came out. After a moment, the sidhe took pity on her.

"These Fae are part of the group known as Forsaken." The little shape-shifter gestured to the ragged band of warriors arrayed around Len. "They puzzled out what the rest of us did not—that if the Hunt could be lured into the caverns beneath Chaima, the world tree's roots might reabsorb it, easing the imbalance between Dhuinne's creative and destructive magic. So that is what we did. Now that the Wild Hunt has been reintegrated with the Mother's magic, it acts in its own best interest. In other words... the best interest of Dhuinne."

Shock flashed across the Magistrate's delicate features.

One of the surviving Unseelie managed to regain the power of speech. "And the best interest of Dhuinne is to *murder one-quarter of the Fae Court*?"

Albigard twisted around, fixing the man with a perfectly bland stare. "Clearly so."

The Unseelie sputtered with outrage.

"Oren has long sacrificed Dhuinne's wellbeing in favor of his own lust for power," Albigard continued coldly. "He has been working behind the scenes for years to destabilize the Fae realm. And now, he is dead at the Hunt's hands—along, presumably, with those who secretly supported his schemes."

"Which brings us neatly to another issue," said the cat-sidhe.

"*Two* issues," Albigard corrected, and Len caught his breath as he realized this could finally be their chance to right a wrong that he had come to accept might be unrightable.

"Three issues," Danon growled, because apparently the Forsaken had some grievances to air as well.

Little wonder, really.

The Magistrate looked warily between Albigard, the cat-sidhe, and the Forsaken. "To what do you refer?"

The sidhe crossed their arms. "First. The imbalance in Dhuinne's magical fields long preceded the Hunt going rogue. In fact, it began not long after the conclusion of the Last Great War... when the Court started sending Unseelie to Earth to rule the humans from behind the scenes."

Len watched with interest as the Magistrate looked blank for a long moment... only for slow realization to widen her eyes.

"Are you implying..." she began, only to trail off as other members of the Court began to exchange startled looks.

"I'm doing more than implying it," the sidhe replied.

Albigard took up the thread. "Interestingly, it took a human to deduce an answer so obvious that no one in the Fae realm had stumbled upon it in more than two hundred years." His gaze brushed Len's, softening infinitesimally before once more turning cold. "Our people have been sending Unseelie to another realm by the thousands, only to wring our hands afterward, and bemoan the fact that the creative and destructive elements of Dhuinne were falling out of balance."

The self-possessed Magistrate was *genuinely gaping* at Albigard's words, her perfect lips parted as the truth hit home.

"The Unseelie on Earth must be recalled," Albigard continued mercilessly, "or Chaima will topple and Dhuinne will fall into chaos."

"Impossible!" cried one of the Unseelie from the group on the floor—not Teague, Len noted.

Albigard's green gaze fell on the man like a heavy weight. "You think so?" he asked pointedly.

"In that case, I would urge you to take up your objections with the Hunt."

The Unseelie's eyes flicked nervously to the dark cloud roiling behind the Forsaken. His jaw snapped shut.

"The second matter," Albigard continued, "relates to a provision of the treaty with the demons. The survival of Ransley Thorpe, the last vampire left alive at the time, was one condition of the peace agreement. He and his soul-mate Zorah Bright were killed by the Hunt while attempting to help close one of the damaged areas in the veil between realms. Killed... by a Fae creature."

The Magistrate appeared to have regained some of her composure.

"That is deeply regrettable," she said. "But surely the matter is beyond redress at this point."

"Not necessarily," Albigard said. "Both vampires were bound to the demon known as Nigellus. If he could retrieve their souls from the Endless Void, it might yet be possible to save them."

Several of the Court members appeared taken aback.

"Is such a thing truly possible?" asked another of the Seelie.

The cat-sidhe huffed out a breath. "Perhaps. It appears this one will not speak of it himself" — they indicated Albigard — "but he volunteered as bait to draw the Hunt to Chaima... and he died for it."

Len couldn't suppress his shiver as he remembered warm lips turning cold and still beneath his own.

"Dhuinne acknowledged his sacrifice," the sidhe went on, "and returned his soul to his body as repayment. If Chaima could channel his essence back from the Void after the Hunt consumed it, perhaps the demon can do the same for his vampire wards."

Please, Len thought. *Please, let that be true.*

"For what, precisely, are you asking?" the Magistrate demanded.

"The demon Nigellus must be allowed to enter Dhuinne with the bodies of Ransley Thorpe and Zorah Bright," Albigard said in an absolutely flat tone. "After which he must be given access to the Hunt, and possibly to Chaima, so that he may attempt to use them as a conduit to wherever the vampires' souls currently reside."

Muttered conversation rose in the background, the tone sounding somewhere between shocked and scandalized.

"Unless you'd prefer to explain to the Demon Council why you were unwilling to even *attempt* restitution for a blatant treaty violation," the cat-sidhe added helpfully.

The conversation faded away to silence.

The Magistrate traded speaking looks with several other Court members before turning back to Albigard.

"We are willing to take up these two topics for debate and a vote, given the rather extraordinary circumstances at play," she said. "What is the third provision?"

Nezri and Danon stepped forward, heads held high.

"Diplomatic liaison and full amnesty for the Forsaken," Nezri said.

"No more attacks on us," Danon put in. "No more bounties on our heads."

Albigard let that sink in for a moment, and raised a slow eyebrow at the Magistrate. "As you contemplate the matter, you might consider recent events. Doubtless the guards who escaped the aftermath of this morning's raid gave a full report of what happened to their fellows."

"The Hunt killed them," Danon spelled out, "and spared us. I expect that means Dhuinne wants us alive, and won't take kindly to anyone who wants us dead just because we refuse to accept your laws or your rule."

"There's a higher law now," Nezri finished. The Hunt coiled behind her, silently menacing.

"So... it would appear," the Magistrate said slowly.

"Make your decisions," Albigard told her, rising and heading for the stairs leading down from the dais. "But before you do, ask yourself who you really serve. Do you serve Dhuinne and all her creatures? Or do you only serve yourselves?"

Silence followed him as he rejoined Len and the others. The cat-sidhe gave a small, satisfied smile before hopping nimbly from the dais and joining them as well.

Somewhat to Len's surprise, Teague intercepted them to offer the use of nearby accommodations while they awaited the court's decision. He approached Albigard with one hand raised to halt him, and Albigard stopped to speak with him as Len hovered a couple of steps away, watching the exchange warily.

"You should know that everything I did, I did because I thought it best for our people, and for our realm," Teague said.

"Clearly the Hunt concurs with your assessment," Albigard replied neutrally, still wrapped in his armor of chilly detachment.

Teague gave him a single nod in return, and addressed Len. "Human. It was you who unraveled the clues behind Dhuinne's growing chaos."

"Yes," Len agreed, even though it hadn't been phrased as a question.

The Fae looked like he was struggling with something that tasted bad, but he finally said, "Thank you."

Len shrugged, and resisted the very natural urge to punch him in the face again. "Don't mention it."

Half an hour later, they were installed in a borrowed cottage near the edge of what seemed to be a residential district—based on what could be seen of it beyond the choking plant life, anyway. Most of the Forsaken had returned to their camp, but Danon and Nezri stayed behind with Len, Albigard, and the cat-sidhe to wait for the Court's verdict.

The fact that the Hunt had remained in the Court chamber rather than following them made Len cautiously optimistic that the Fae ruling body would do the right thing in the end. Albigard had asked them whether they served Dhuinne or themselves. The truth was, those two options had just become more or less the same thing—failing to serve Dhuinne now brought immediate and deadly consequences.

If something like this had happened on Earth, Len might have been appalled. There were some big implications when it came to the concept of free will, for one thing. But under the current circumstances? He didn't give one single, solitary fuck about it, as long as it meant the Court did what Len and the others wanted them to do.

He was done with living in this constant state of crisis. *Done.*

The twins took one look around the neat little faerie cottage where the five of them had been installed, and headed outside to hang out in the overgrown back yard instead. The sidhe also gave the place a quick onceover before promptly shifting into cat form, and curling up in a sunbeam.

Len took in Albigard's brittle appearance with a measuring glance. There were only two interior doors inside the cottage. With a steadying hand on his lower back, Len urged Albigard toward the closest one, which thankfully opened onto a small bedroom containing a bed and a side table. He closed the door behind them. The Fae blinked at the room as though he'd never seen such a thing before. Concerned, Len lifted a hand to Albigard's jaw and turned his head with a touch until their eyes met.

"Hey," he said softly, not sure how close his companion was to a breakdown after watching his only remaining parent die, and then having to pretend not to care. "Your father... you can still mourn him, you know."

Albigard's eyes slid closed. The tension of maintaining control etched lines into his chiseled face. "Please don't," he whispered.

Len let his breath flow out slowly, and dropped his hand. "All right." He looked around the room, and ended up sinking down to sit on the floor, using the side of the bed as a backrest. Sleep wasn't in the cards yet, but he was undeniably wrecked. They both were.

After several long moments, Albigard sank down next to him with effortless Fae grace. Len reached into the space between them, offering his hand palm-up without looking over at his companion. Another pause, and Albigard took it. His skin was still icy cold with shock. Len tangled their fingers together and held firm, not commenting on the fine tremor he could feel thrumming through the contact.

They sat in silence like that for what Len thought was probably a couple of hours. Albigard flinched as a soft knock sounded at the door. Len gave his hand a final reassuring squeeze and clambered to his feet to see who it was. When he opened the door, however, it was to find a platter sitting on the floor outside. The large plate was piled with bread, cheese, cold meat, and something that looked like a bunch of grapes but probably wasn't. Next to it stood what looked suspiciously like a dusty wine bottle.

Len picked up the items and brought them inside.

"I think the cat-sidhe is trying to feed us," he said. "Is it still okay for me to eat and drink this?"

Albigard's gaze remained distant and dazed, but he did at least meet Len's eyes. "As I have told you repeatedly, you are already mine. No other Fae may claim you." He paused. "Though you might want to go lightly with the mead."

Len gave up trying to deny the surge of warmth that followed the words. It tightened something low in his gut—an unconscious response to a possessive Fae staking his claim.

"Good to know," he said. "On both counts."

He set the platter and bottle between them and started eating, giving Albigard pointed looks until the Fae reluctantly did the same. Predictably, it was the best damned food Len had ever eaten, and the mead should definitely have come with its own warning label.

Albigard accepted the bottle from Len and tipped it up, his pale throat working as he took a few swallows before lowering it.

"This is a similar vintage to the drink I used to trick the demonkin into a gift-bond, in the early days of our acquaintance," he mused. "I fear I underestimated its effects on a metabolism that was, at the time, largely human."

It took a moment for Len to realize he was talking about Zorah.

"You got Zorah drunk on faerie mead?" Len asked, the dull ache of speaking about her now overshadowed by the sharper ache of hesitant hope.

"It was... not an experience either of us would ever wish to repeat," Albigard replied. "She gets very..." He trailed off, clearly searching for the right word and coming up blank.

"I can only imagine," Len said, and waved the bottle away when Albigard offered it back to him. The stuff was spreading warmth all through Len's body after only a few sips, and wasn't bringing on the wash of black depression that usually made it easy for him to say no to booze.

Dangerous. Or... y'know... potentially awesome. But not when they were waiting for word on the Court's decision, and Len might need his wits about him. Albigard set the bottle aside, probably for the same reason. They concentrated on the food instead, finishing it in fairly short order.

More time passed, and a new knock came — this time at the front door. Len exchanged a look with his companion and they both rose, entering the main room at the same time as Danon and Nezri, who must have heard the new arrival as well.

The cat-sidhe opened the door, revealing a Seelie in formal attire who gave a stiff nod and did not ask to enter. "Elder. I have been dispatched by the Court to inform you that decisions have been reached in the matters of the demon Nigellus, and relations with the group known as the Forsaken."

"And what are those decisions?" the sidhe asked, when the messenger did not immediately continue.

"You may arrange for the demon's admittance to Dhuinne, with a small retinue to transport the bodies of Ransley Thorpe and Zorah Bright," the woman said in a wooden tone. "They will have the Court's guarantee of safe passage to and from the gate to Earth. Additionally, a joint committee is to be commissioned. It will address issues related to the Forsaken. The Court has determined that the Forsaken may nominate their own members to form one-half of said committee."

Len's heart leapt.

"And how many more members of the Court succumbed to the Hunt during the negotiations?" the cat-sidhe asked, as casually as though they were discussing sports scores or the latest reality TV show.

"Three," the Fae woman said stiffly. "Two from the Unseelie side, and one from the Seelie."

"I imagine that would be highly motivational," the cat-sidhe replied. "What of the question regarding the recall of the Unseelie operatives from the human realm?"

"Still under debate," said the messenger. "It appears the discussion may stretch over multiple days."

"Hmm. Brave of them," the sidhe observed. "Very well. You may tell the Magistrate that I will see to the demon's arrival in short order. Please ensure that the guards and the warden of the gateway are informed."

NINETEEN

The messenger gave another stiff bow and departed. When she was gone, the sidhe turned to Len, Albigard, and the twins. "It appears I have a task to complete. As there is no further cause for delay, I will depart now. Rest assured, I shall return as soon as possible and keep you informed of the details."

Albigard took a deep, shuddering breath. "Thank you, Elder."

The cat-sidhe gave him a quicksilver smile. "Remain strong for a little longer, Albigard of the Unseelie. All may yet come out as it should."

With that, the sidhe transformed into a cat and trotted out the door. Len stepped forward and closed it behind them, feeling a bit numb.

The twins shared a look. Nezri turned to Albigard and spoke. "We should go to our people with this news. Will you be all right here alone? If you prefer, you are welcome to come with us."

"Your offer is kind," Albigard told her, "but the cat-sidhe will return here first when they have something to report."

Danon shrugged. "As you like. Just so you know, the offer's always open. We'll be returning to the main camp in a couple of days, at a guess. So you know where to find us if you need us."

Albigard managed a thin smile. "I would not presume to believe I could breach your wards so easily."

"Pfft. They'll be open to you, Unseelie," Danon replied. His eyes flicked to Len. "And you as well, human. Couldn't really have one without the other, after all."

The spike of feeling that rose in response to that casual declaration took Len by surprise, tightening his throat.

"Thank you," Albigard said.

"Yes. Thank you," Len echoed faintly.

"Fair winds," Nezri said. "Doubtless we will see you again in the course of things."

She opened a portal, and the pair stepped through it. A moment later it snapped shut, and the silence grew very... *complete*. Len blinked a couple of times.

"Right," he said slowly. "On a scale of one to ten, how likely is the world to end if we fall asleep for a bit? Because I get the impression we're in something of a lull, at least temporarily."

Albigard's shoulders sagged. "I wouldn't even care to speculate." His tone was one of utter exhaustion.

"The cat-sidhe's dealing with Nigellus," Len reasoned. "The twins are dealing with the Forsaken. The Court's still busy fighting over the Unseelie presence on Earth, and will be for quite a while. To me, that says there's nothing left for us to do right now. Agreed?"

A pause, then, "... agreed."

"Okay. Good. In that case, we're sleeping. Come on."

There was no lock on the inside of the front door — but there *was* a bar, so Len barred it. Albigard let himself be shepherded back to the bedroom. It was only mid-afternoon, but Len didn't care.

He pushed the Fae onto the bed and followed him down. They were both fully clothed, and Len intended to stay that way in case someone else knocked on the door. The bed was narrow. Maybe that would have been a problem under different circumstances. Right now, it wasn't.

Len pressed close and wrapped his arms around Albigard's unresisting form. The Fae buried his face against Len's shoulder, and five minutes later, he was asleep. Len followed soon after... the feeling of a living body next to him combining with the smell of sunshine and ozone to keep his nightmares at bay.

———◆———

A hand on his shoulder woke Len to darkness, broken only by the glow from a small ball of magical illumination floating in the corner of the room.

"The cat-sidhe has returned," Albigard told him.

Len grunted and tried to get his head on straight. He'd slept straight through the sound of the sidhe's arrival, not to mention Albigard untangling himself and leaving the bed.

"I'm up," he mumbled, needing two attempts before he managed to suit action to words.

God... forget sleeping for a week. Len was going to sleep for a freaking *year* when all this was over. The cottage was quiet as Len stumbled to the bedroom door and into the front room, where the sidhe was waiting as promised.

"The demon and his retinue will be arriving shortly," said the shape-shifter. "I thought you might wish to be present to meet them at the gateway."

"Yes," Albigard replied. "Thank you."

Len rubbed at his face. "When you say 'retinue'..."

The cat-sidhe gave him a small smile. "I believe he was able to procure the assistance of two individuals with a degree of resistance to Dhuinne's influence — another vampire, and a human with natural magic."

His breath caught, his gaze flying to Albigard's. "Guthrie and Vonnie. Will that be all right? Didn't you say their presence here could cause problems?"

The sidhe replied with apparent unconcern. "The Court agreed to grant access to additional people to assist with the transport of the vampires' bodies."

"They did not specify who those people needed to be," Albigard finished.

"Good enough for me," Len said, still feeling only half awake. He ran his hands through his hair, knowing that he probably looked like a disheveled zombie and figuring that no one involved was likely to care. "Are we leaving now?"

"Yes," the sidhe replied. "I want to be present upon their arrival, to prevent the possibility of misunderstandings."

Len suppressed a shudder. "Good plan."

"There is a sink with a hand pump," Albigard said, "if you'd care to splash some water on your face first. And a privy behind the cottage."

"*Thank you,*" Len told him in relief. "Give me, like, two minutes."

He hurried off to take care of some basic needs, mildly amused by the fact that Albigard's glowing magical nightlight followed him around like a helium balloon on a string. Len rejoined the others shortly — privied, washed, and rehydrated after his small adventure with Fae mead a few hours ago.

"Come," the sidhe told them, and opened a portal.

Len followed the others through and found himself on an overgrown hillside lit by blazing torches. This had to be the hill next to the gateway between realms, though it had a totally different appearance at night — and when Len wasn't busy being tackled by angry Fae guards.

The guards were still there, of course. They didn't look much happier to see Albigard now than they had then. Fortunately, the presence of the cat-sidhe, combined with the edict from the Court, appeared to be enough to prevent a repeat of the events of their first visit.

The sidhe marched up to one of the Unseelie. Len was ninety-nine percent sure it was the same guy who'd punched Albigard in the teeth.

"Greetings, guardsman," they said. "My companions and I will await the arrival of the demon and his retinue. You have received your instructions from the Court, I assume?"

"Yes, Elder," the guardsman said grudgingly.

The cat-sidhe nodded in acknowledgement and returned to stand with Len and Albigard. They waited there, in something of a wary standoff, until the first hint of lavender tinted the horizon. Finally, a white glow appeared in mid-air. It widened into a spiral—following the shape of the carving in the wall of the Mound of the Hostages on Earth's side of the gate.

The glow strengthened, becoming so bright Len had to look away. Afterimages danced behind his eyelids. When he managed to blink his vision clear, the white light was gone, and three figures stood among the windswept grass, illuminated by flickering torchlight.

No... not three figures. *Five.*

Nigellus and Guthrie Leonides stood side by side, each with a limp figure cradled in his arms. Vonnie stood on Guthrie's other side, her fingers wrapped around her emerald pendant, a look of intense concentration on her pretty features.

Around them, the Fae guards grasped their weapons tightly, shoulders tense.

"Stand down, all of you," said the leader, speaking with clear reluctance.

Daeana—the Seelie warden of the gateway—stepped out, joining them. "The demon and his companions are guests of the Court," she said, in a tone that brooked no opposition.

"Thank you, Warden," Nigellus said, in his suave, resonant voice. "The Court's cooperation in this matter is greatly appreciated."

From the wry eyebrow she raised, Len didn't get the impression that demonic charm was the way to Daeana's heart.

"I will be accompanying you during your stay, Hellspawn," she declared coolly. "I trust your visit to Dhuinne will be both brief and productive." She turned her attention back to the leader of the Unseelie guards. "Take my post on the other side of the gate until Lianette arrives to relieve you."

The leader gave a stiff bow and moved to obey his orders. With the tension at least somewhat abated, Vonnie hurried forward and enveloped Len in a hug. He closed his eyes and hugged her back tightly.

"You're all right," she breathed. "Both of you. And you did it!"

"We have done nothing as of yet," Albigard said. "That duty will fall to Nigellus."

Vonnie pulled back from Len and sent Albigard a watery smile. "No... you did your part, or we wouldn't be here in the first place. I'm so glad you're both safe."

Daeana had watched the exchange neutrally, but now she lifted her chin, regarding Albigard. "No longer a prisoner, I see. You *have* been busy, son of Oren."

Len flinched inwardly at the mention of Albigard's father, but the Fae had once more donned his icy armor.

"Perhaps you would conduct us to a place where we may proceed with our guests' purpose here, Warden," was all he said in reply.

The faintest hint of a smile curled one corner of Daeana's lips in the firelight. "Of course."

The cat-sidhe gave Nigellus and the others an assessing look. Len's attention fell on Guthrie, holding Zorah cradled against his broad chest. He frowned, distracted by the slowly expanding circle of blackened and dying grass around the vampire's feet.

Vonnie followed his gaze. "It's a vampire thing. Don't worry about it," she said. "So, we're going now?"

"Indeed," said the sidhe. "I believe the Wild Hunt remains in the Court's inner chamber. It should be empty otherwise, since that august body will not reconvene for several hours yet. We will go there and see what can be done."

This was apparently too much for the leader of the guards, who straightened in outrage. "You would take a *demon* to the inner seat of Fae power?" he demanded, aghast.

Daeana turned a cold eye on him. "As those are my orders, given by the very Court you are so eager to defend — yes, I would," she said blandly.

The sidhe opened a portal, once more cutting through the layered protections surrounding the Court building as though they weren't there. Albigard stepped through, and the sidhe gestured

Nigellus and the others to do the same. Len followed after Vonnie, and the cat-sidhe brought up the rear.

The echoing space on the other side of the portal was dark, and smelled of the ever-present perfumed flowering vines that covered so much of Dhuinne. Vonnie reached for Len's arm as the flickering light of the portal extinguished, and they steadied each other in the dark until Daeana murmured a few low words. The huge flowers hanging all around the chamber began to glow with bioluminescence, casting pale blue light across everything.

Well... everything except the roiling black mass of oily smoke, covering the empty space where petitioners usually stood before the Court dais.

Daeana stared at the Wild Hunt rather fixedly for a few moments.

"That," she said, "is *decidedly* disconcerting."

The cat-sidhe walked forward. "As I know you to be one who serves Dhuinne faithfully, you are in no danger from the Hunt."

Nigellus also eyed the Fae archetype of death hovering quiescent before them. "It does appear somewhat... diminished, compared to the last time I encountered it." He shifted the burden in his arms, and Len got a good look at Ransley Thorpe for the first time since staring into his sightless blue eyes during the battle in St. Louis.

Not to put too fine a point on it, both Rans and Zorah looked way too good for having been dead so long. Nigellus, on the other hand, didn't look so hot. It made Len wonder if the demon had been pouring power into their bodies this entire time to keep them from decaying.

"Did the cat-sidhe inform you of the events beneath the world-tree?" Albigard asked. "I am uncertain whether this would be better attempted there."

"I have received a report on the matter, yes." Nigellus moved to one of the overgrown benches in the gallery and carefully placed Rans' body on it. Guthrie followed suit, placing Zorah on the bench next to him, with their heads lying close together.

"Putting aside the rather fascinating concept of the legendary Chaima being a real, physical place," the demon continued, "it sounds as though the circumstances surrounding your resurrection were somewhat different. The roots of the world tree did not absorb Ransley and Ms. Bright's essences. The Hunt flung them directly into the realm you call the Endless Void."

"I do not think Chaima can help the process, in this instance," the cat-sidhe agreed. "Either the demon will be able to access the Void through the Hunt, or he won't."

"Next question," Len asked, unable to help himself. "Is the Hunt likely to think that having a demon poking around in its guts is in the best interest of Dhuinne?"

"That," Albigard said grimly, "is a very interesting question."

"I will attempt to convey the context," the sidhe said, and went to commune with the damned cloud while Daeana looked on curiously.

"If it helps prevent the resumption of war," the Seelie warden observed, "it would appear to be in *everyone's* best interest."

"I couldn't agree more," said Nigellus.

Freed of the burden of Zorah's body, Guthrie came over and put a hand on Len's shoulder in greeting, before focusing his attention on Vonnie.

"You holding up okay?" he asked quietly.

She nodded. "I'm fine, I told you. Dhuinne's influence was only a problem when I was too exhausted to keep my eyes open. I'll warn you if it becomes an issue, Leo. Until then, please don't fuss."

Aside from a weird sort of background hum, Len hadn't noticed any of the effects that made Dhuinne such a fearsome place to outsiders. But without her magic, Vonnie would be vulnerable to its mind-twisting powers... and the way Guthrie's vampire aura interacted to wilt the rampaging plant life around him was frankly creepy. Nigellus seemed unaffected by his surroundings at first glance, but as Len looked away, he thought for a moment that he saw the ghostly outline of massive, leathery wings in the corner of his vision.

The cat-sidhe straightened away from the coiling edge of the Hunt. "I've done what I can. Unfortunately, the circumstances are a bit more complicated than simple self-preservation."

Daeana snorted. "Well, on the positive side, it's not as though it can kill him."

"True," Nigellus agreed, dry as dust. "Now... if I may proceed?"

The sidhe stepped aside with a little *be-my-guest* flourish, and the demon took their place. The Wild Hunt coiled restlessly, as though wary of the enemy it had tangled with once before, in St. Louis. Vonnie curled one hand around Len's arm, and the other around Guthrie's. Guthrie covered it with his, squeezing. Len glanced at Albigard and found the Fae's green gaze shining with tightly restrained hope. The Fae crossed his arms; his shoulders a tense line as he turned to watch Nigellus work.

The powerful demon of fate reached a hand into the dark mass, just as the cat-sidhe had done before. It recoiled from him, only to surge back an instant later, enveloping his arm to the shoulder. Nigellus clenched his jaw, and Len blinked as ghostly ram's horns phased in and out from the sides of his skull for a few seconds before disappearing.

They remained locked that way for long minutes. Nigellus' eyes glowed hellfire-red in the low light. The Hunt writhed and twisted, neither attacking nor fleeing. It was nerve-wracking to watch — all the more so because Len had absolutely no clue what was *actually happening*. He kept throwing glances at Albigard in hopes of gaining some kind of insight from the Fae, but his pale face might as well have been cut from marble.

More time passed, and Nigellus grunted, going down on a knee. Vonnie twitched hard, her grip on Len's arm tightening. For his part, Len tried not to make assumptions when he didn't understand jack shit about what was going on... but that hadn't looked good. His suspicion was confirmed a few moments later, when the cat-sidhe made a small noise of disappointment.

"He does not have the power," said the shape-shifter.

Albigard let out a low, hissing breath.

And... no.

Just, *no*.

Something cold and implacable rose in Len's chest. A solid wave of *nope* that wasn't content to stand by and watch Nigellus fail after all they'd been through to get here. Before Len truly understood what was happening, an icy rush of power sank through his skin, only to explode out of him in the next moment... aimed straight at the demon.

TWENTY

Vonnie jerked her hand away from Len's arm in the instant before the crackling blue energy hit Nigellus. The Hunt flinched from the blast of death energy. The demon did not. The lightning-blast of power sank into him, and Nigellus gritted his teeth. He reached deeper into the swirling mass of blackness, the tendons in his neck standing out. Horns and wings burst from the demon's body, which seemed to swell with bulk and muscle. Tailored clothing tore.

With a low growl of determination, the terrifying nightmare creature—who'd been a suave man in a business suit mere seconds ago—closed his fist around something intangible and *yanked*.

The Wild Hunt howled in surprise, swirling away to coalesce near one corner of the chamber's vaulted ceiling. Which, Len supposed, was a preferable response to freaking out and killing everyone in the chamber.

Nigellus' massive chest rose and fell. His lips remained in their feral snarl, revealing teeth that were very… *pointy*. He was braced on a hand and a knee, and he wasn't getting up.

"Someone help me to the bodies," he ground out.

Guthrie and Albigard hurried forward—which was just as well, since Len might have been able to support one giant wing on, y'know, *a good day*. Which this wasn't. In fact, he felt like his knees were about to give way after loosing that unexpected blast of magical power. The three figures staggered down the aisle to the benches where Zorah and Rans' bodies were laid out. Nigellus reached a clawed hand out to each of the vampires' foreheads, grasping their skulls.

Several moments passed, and the demon fell to his knees. One wing flopped into the aisle, while the other draped sloppily over the back of the bench in front of him. His hands slid away from the pair's heads.

"It is done," he said, while Len tried to decide how much mental capacity to devote to hope, and how much to the faintly hysterical voice jabbering, *oh my god, what the hell did I just do?*

Zorah and Rans still lay unmoving. No breath expanded their lungs; no pulse throbbed in their carotid arteries. But, then... it wouldn't, would it? They were vampires.

Daeana had watched the proceedings with crossed arms and a neutral expression. Now, she raised an eyebrow, tilting her head as she examined the collapsed demon. "Such a pity this opportunity did not arise during the war. I think if we were quick enough, we could get him dismembered and the pieces packed in salt before he recovered," she said to the cat-sidhe.

"I would advise against trying," the sidhe replied wryly. "And not only because of the Court's guarantee of safe passage."

The warden hummed a reluctant noise of agreement. Then her gaze raked over Len before landing on Albigard. "On a related note, you failed to mention that the human vassal you dragged with you to the Fae realm was also a necromancer, son of Oren."

Albigard's expression turned flinty. "I strongly suggest forgetting you saw that, Warden."

"Whereas I would ask you to remember that the human also played a pivotal role in saving Dhuinne," the cat-sidhe added. "I doubt the Hunt would take it kindly if harm came to him."

Daeana gave them all a grim smile. "Oh, don't worry. It's more than my job's worth — on both counts."

With Guthrie and Albigard arrayed watchfully by Nigellus' side, the demon took a deep breath and closed his eyes. His horns and wings retracted, his bulk diminishing until a striking, human-looking man in torn clothing sprawled next to the vampires' unmoving bodies. He rose, bracing himself on the benches for a moment before straightening to his full height.

"May we have no cause to meet on the battlefield in the foreseeable future, Warden," he said. "That is, after all, the goal of this entire exercise."

"Did it work, though?" Vonnie blurted.

Nigellus looked down at the pair lying on the bench. "Their souls once more reside in their bodies. It is as well they are bound together — I would not have been able to seek them separately." His whiskey-brown eyes fell on Len, no longer glowing with hellfire. "In fact, I would not have been able to retrieve them at all without the extra power. They owe their lives to you."

The words skittered across Len's mind like water on an orange peel, not really penetrating. Still, everyone was looking at him as if he was expected to respond somehow.

"I don't even understand what I did," he said, deflecting. "But, if it helped them, I'm... glad?"

He sought out Albigard, hoping for a helping hand, or at least some kind of distraction and change of subject. The Fae returned his gaze with one that was visibly fond, which only succeeded in making Len feel even more flustered.

Fortunately, Guthrie saved him.

"I assume the inner sanctum of the Fae Court isn't an appropriate venue for these two to recover from having their souls shoved back in their bodies," he said. "Is there someplace private we can stay until they're in a condition to be transported back to Earth?" He raised an eyebrow at Nigellus. "What about it? Do they just need to rest now, or what?"

The demon took another deep breath. "Yes, I daresay it will take a few hours for them to regain their mental bearings and realize they're corporeal again. When they wake up, they'll need to feed, but they should be all right otherwise."

"That's why I'm here," Guthrie replied. "Vampire blood bank. It will heal them faster than human blood would."

"As long as you don't start sniffing around any Fae blood, nightwalker," Daeana said pointedly.

"Fae blood is disgusting," Guthrie replied, without missing a beat. He smiled, revealing a hint of fang. "Go on... ask me how I know."

"Oh, my god. Could we not right now?" Vonnie asked. "Please?"

"Seconded," Len agreed, in no mood for any more inter-species pissing matches after the last few weeks.

"I will take them back to the accommodations the Court offered us," said the cat-sidhe. "They may recover there."

"And as soon as they do, we'll all be out of your hair," Guthrie put in. "I don't think anyone here is in a hurry to extend their travel visa."

"Perhaps the warden would agree to escort me back to the gateway immediately," Nigellus said. "My presence in this realm is already unwelcome, and I suspect my presence at the vampires' bedsides would be doubly so."

It seemed like a century ago, but Len remembered the battle in St. Louis. Nigellus had frozen the vampires in place, physically preventing them from going to Albigard's aid when he'd been captured. With that in mind, the demon was probably right.

"As you like, Hellspawn," Daeana agreed, readily enough. She shot the cat-sidhe a look. "I assume you can contain three vampires, a necromancer, and a human adept without assistance, Elder."

"I expect I'll muddle through somehow," the cat-sidhe agreed.

Daeana shrugged, after giving the Wild Hunt a final, wary look, she gestured with exaggerated courtly elegance to Nigellus, indicating he should precede her.

The demon turned and gave the rest of them a nod of acknowledgement, looking pale to the point of translucence after whatever powers he'd drained to return Rans and Zorah's souls to their bodies.

"Until we meet again," he said, and left with his escort.

"Well," Guthrie said, once they'd gone. "That was exciting. And that demon bastard had better be right about these two waking up, or there's going to be serious hell to pay." He paused. "So to speak."

"I would trust the word of a demon of fate when it comes to souls and their disposition," the cat-sidhe assured them, before opening a new portal.

"If you say so." Guthrie leaned down to gather Zorah into his arms again. "Albigard, can you manage all right with this asshole?" He tilted his chin at Rans.

"I will manage," Albigard said softly, and hauled the vampire's limp body into a fireman's carry.

Vonnie took Len's hand, and the motley group stepped through the cat-sidhe's portal, leaving the Wild Hunt behind.

Once they arrived, the cat-sidhe claimed a need to deal with important business elsewhere and promised to return in a few hours. Len hadn't bothered to check behind the second interior door in their borrowed cottage earlier—but as it turned out, it opened into another, larger bedroom containing two beds. While not exactly spacious, there was at least enough room for the six of them to squeeze in without being on top of each other.

Guthrie and Albigard placed Zorah and Rans on the beds. Len and Vonnie settled into a couple of chairs they'd borrowed from the front room, crammed into the space between the wall and the footboards. Guthrie settled on the edge of his granddaughter's mattress, while Albigard perched next to his on-again, off-again frenemy.

And they waited.

"So," Vonnie asked, to fill the silence. "That was necromancy, huh? Guess we should count ourselves lucky you never whipped out the blue lightning bolts when we were sneaking tapas from your kitchen at the Brown Fox."

"It wasn't an issue back then," Len muttered. "And anyway, I can't really control it."

"Oh, *honey*. I feel that pain on a cellular level," Vonnie said. "I could tell you stories…"

"Get her to tell you about the apartment fire sometime," Guthrie offered from the bed.

Vonnie glared at him. "*Not that story*." She returned her attention to Len. "Seriously, though. It gets better. You can learn to how use it properly, with practice."

Len wasn't at all sure he wanted more practice with necromancy. Not when it meant being exposed to a constant parade of death.

"I guess so," he said, and changed the subject. "Look... I don't know if I really want to hear the answer to this, but... did the Hunt do any more damage on Earth while we were chasing our tails here in Dhuinne? It took us a few days to get the thing contained, and I just kept thinking about how much destruction it might have caused in that amount of time."

Vonnie's expression grew serious. "It's... not great news. But it could have been a lot worse. We've only got what information we could find on the international news sites from Ireland, but as far as the reporting goes, it destroyed an irregular area of about twenty square miles west of Chicago."

Len's breathing stuttered.

Vonnie hurried on. "Seriously, though—it wasn't as bad as you might expect from that. Most of the area had already been evacuated when it broke through the veil, and around the edges where it hadn't been evacuated yet, they still had a bit of warning. A lot of people got out okay."

He fought lightheadedness. "How many didn't?"

Vonnie took a deep breath and let it out slowly. "About eight hundred and fifty, at last count. But... Len. It could have headed east and ended up in the city itself. There could have been thousands dead. Tens of thousands."

There could have been, yes. But *eight hundred and fifty people...*

He turned to Albigard, not even sure why, but the Fae wouldn't meet his eyes. He'd been completely silent since leaving the Court chamber, and there was a brittle tension to the line of his back that Len didn't much like the look of. If they'd been alone, Len would have gone to him. With the others here, he wasn't at all sure the gesture would be appreciated. Honestly, he had no idea how Albigard felt about the prospect of being outed to the small group of people who nominally considered him a friend. It had never occurred to him to ask.

So he sat in his chair, squashed together with Vonnie in the cramped space, and fretted.

What if the vampires didn't wake up?

What if they woke up, but they weren't okay?

What if the death toll on Earth was way worse than the authorities were letting on?

What if Daeana and Nigellus got into a fight on the way back to the gate and managed to start another war?

He hauled off and mentally smacked himself upside the head before his thoughts could spiral any further.

Enough.

He *really* wished Albigard didn't look like he was one stiff breeze away from shattering into sharp-edged pieces, though.

Silence settled over the little group. Guthrie idly took Zorah's hand between both of his, running his thumb back and forth over her skin. Vonnie leaned her shoulder against Len's with a reassuring pressure, which he appreciated more than he could say. Albigard stared fixedly at

Ransley Thorpe's slack face, though Len wasn't at all sure that he was truly seeing it.

Outside, the sun rose, the angle of the light changing gradually as the morning progressed. Hours passed, and Len was appalled to find himself beginning to doze off, as the events of the past several days caught up with him. He jerked back to awareness when Guthrie inhaled sharply, because *vampires didn't need to breathe.* Vonnie straightened in her chair next to him.

"Leo?" she prompted.

"I felt her hand twitch," Guthrie said.

TWENTY-ONE

Len leaned forward. Albigard stared down at Rans with an intensity so laser-like it could have burned through steel. After a few moments, the dark-haired vampire stirred and groaned.

"*Bloody...*" The weak curse trailed off. One hand lifted to his forehead as though to combat a headache, and Rans rolled awkwardly into a sitting position. "Please tell me someone got the license number of whatever lorry just hit me—"

Albigard watched him, frozen. On the other bed, Zorah gave a pitiful moan, and Guthrie helped her upright, gathering her against his chest.

"Zorah?" Rans asked sharply, his eyes flying to her.

"It's all right," Guthrie said. "She's all right, Rans. I've got her."

Rans relaxed, his expression softening. Vonnie's hand fumbled for Len's and he took it, returning her hard squeeze as relief hit him in a hot wave.

Meanwhile, Rans had regained enough of his bearings to notice Albigard sitting on his other side, statue-like. He blinked. "A bedside vigil, Alby? *Really*? Buggering hell, now I *know* it was bad. What on Earth happened to—"

Albigard grabbed two fistfuls of Rans' black henley and buried his face against the vampire's shoulder. Dark eyebrows shot up, and Len was treated to the first instance he could ever recall of Ransley Thorpe, seven-hundred-year-old creature of the night, being rendered speechless with shock. After a stunned moment, his arms came around Albigard's shoulders, though his expression still held more than a hint of complete bewilderment.

The Fae curled further into him, and Len's throat closed up as Albigard's shoulders began to shake. Beside him, Vonnie sniffled. Len let go of her hand in favor of wrapping an arm around her, while trying his best not to start sobbing like a baby because *maybe things were going to be all right now*.

"What happened?" Zorah rasped, still slumped against Guthrie. "Guthrie? You're s'posed to be in Scotland..."

"What's the last thing you remember?" Len asked, thankfully managing to keep his voice steady.

She looked blank. Rans did not. Len watched the slow-dawning realization cross the English vampire's face.

"The Hunt..." he breathed. Then he took a quick inventory of the room, his glacier-blue eyes regaining some of their usual clarity. "Nigellus?"

"He, uh..." Len had to stop and clear his throat. "He kind of... lost you guys for a while. We had to lure the Wild Hunt back to Dhuinne and corral it before he could get your souls back. You've both been dead for... actually, I don't know how long it's been. More than a week, I'm pretty sure. Anyway, he was here earlier, but he left."

"The Fae weren't overwhelmingly thrilled by the idea of having a demon inside Dhuinne," Guthrie explained. "And I gather he's in the doghouse with you two, as well."

"So, let's just say, you've missed some things," Len finished.

Rans hesitated, looking at the Fae in his arms with the air of someone who'd been handed an expensive and breakable gift, but had no earthly idea what he was supposed to do with it.

"Clearly so," he said.

Len took a deep breath, trying to push aside some of the emotion clogging his chest. "But enough about that. I have a serious question now. Albigard, how come you didn't lose your magic the first time you told me you and Rans weren't friends? Because I'm sorry, but that was a blatant, bald-faced lie."

"We are not friends," Albigard said into the vampire's shoulder. His voice was hoarse.

Rans snorted. "*Friends*? Good god. Definitely not. More like… siblings who drive each other utterly mental on a regular basis, I suppose. Speaking of which, this really is becoming rather disconcerting now, Tinkerbell."

"Agreed," said Albigard, making no move to extricate himself.

"Leave him be, Bela," Len told the vampire. "Stuff went down that you don't know about. Some of it was really bad."

Something in Len's tone must have hinted at *how* bad, because the vampire's expression sobered. Albigard finally pulled himself together enough to straighten away from the embrace, drawing his self-possession around him like a tattered cloak.

"Forgive me," he murmured. "I should hate to feel that I'd offended your delicate sensibilities."

"Aww... I think it's sweet," Zorah mumbled. "But I also feel like grade-A shit right now. Otherwise I'd come over there and hug you, too, Tink."

"Please don't feel obligated," Albigard told her.

"You two need blood," Guthrie said, redirecting them toward more practical matters. "Fortunately for you, my jugular is on tap today. Just keep in mind that I only have Vonnie and Len to feed from afterward, and Len already looks like he's about to pass out."

"Somewhat surprisingly," Len told him, "despite having the crap knocked out of me over the past few weeks, my blood volume is fine. Just don't expect me to stay awake afterward, because I'm wrecked."

And he wasn't the only one... but even after all of this, they weren't done. There was still the Court's decision regarding the Unseelie on Earth. Albigard would stay on Dhuinne until that knot had also been unpicked, Len was sure—and Len wasn't inclined to leave him here alone while that happened.

For now, though, all was finally well. And Len tried—honestly *tried*—to soak in that realization without worrying about the rest of it. He accepted an embrace from Zorah, once she'd fed from Guthrie and regained a bit of her strength. Afterward, he offered his vampire ex-boss a vein in his wrist with good grace, and cracked a lame joke about employee benefits. He added a few additions and corrections to Guthrie's rundown of what, exactly, they'd been up to while Rans and Zorah were dead — mostly so Albigard wouldn't be forced to do it.

When that was done, Rans gave Albigard a long look laced with both sympathy and speculation, while Zorah made good on her earlier threat and thoroughly flummoxed the Fae by hugging him, too.

"I know what it's like to lose a father who hurt you," she said quietly. "You're still allowed to grieve, even if it's for things you never really had in the first place."

Albigard submitted to the embrace a bit stiffly. "So I am told," he replied, his gaze catching Len's.

Rans tilted his head, considering them. "Hmm. I think you may have found something, as well as losing something. Am I right, Alby?"

Albigard did not break eye contact with Len. "Perhaps," he said.

The front door opened, and the cat-sidhe entered, breaking the moment.

"Ah," said the shape-shifter, examining the vampires with a look of interest. "You're awake. Good. How was death?"

"We appear to have slept through it," Rans said. "Next time, we'll try to take better notes."

Guthrie leveled a severe frown at him. "No 'next time.' Jesus, I've barely recovered from *this* round."

"Seriously, though," Zorah said. "I guess the clue's probably in the name, but the Endless Void is *boring*. I mean... you remember what it was like before you were born?"

"No," Len said.

"Right," Zorah finished, gesturing at him as though he'd made the point for her. "It was a lot like that."

Len supposed that as potential afterlives went, that was something he could deal with. At least it sounded restful.

"Are we about ready to head back, then?" Vonnie asked. "Because as fascinating as the philosophical implications might be, I'm only going to be able to hold my barrier against Dhuinne's magic for so long."

Guthrie was at her side in an instant. "I shouldn't have drained you. *Damn it...*"

She waved him off with a look of fond exasperation. "*Stop.* I'm not saying I'm two minutes away from mental collapse, Leo. I'm saying we should probably start thinking about an exit strategy."

"I will take you to the gateway now if you wish it," said the cat-sidhe. "Doubtless the Court will be happier once you are all back on Earth."

"They're not the only ones," Guthrie agreed.

"No argument here," Zorah said. "This place doesn't exactly bring back rosy memories."

"Indeed not," Rans added darkly.

Vonnie turned to Len. "How about it, Blue? You ready to blow this popsicle stand?"

He shook his head and took a step back, moving closer to Albigard. "Can't yet, Red. You go on, though."

She gave him a worried look. "You're staying? Len, haven't you done enough already? This place — even if it doesn't drive you mad... it's dangerous. *They're* dangerous." She shot Albigard an apologetic glance. "Sorry, but it's true."

Albigard didn't dispute her words. Neither did the cat-sidhe.

Len offered her a strained smile. "Yeah, I'd noticed. But apparently I've got political clout now... which I freely admit is not a sentence I ever thought I'd hear myself saying."

"*Clout* might be overstating it slightly," Albigard retorted, because even after everything, he was still an asshole at heart.

"The Court's still fighting over what to do about the Unseelie on Earth," Len went on, ignoring him. "That's... kind of a big deal, and there's no one else here to speak for humanity." He paused. "Which is *another* sentence I never thought I'd be saying."

"In that case, I can't think of anyone better suited," Rans said smoothly. "Alby — keep him safe, won't you?"

"You've been dead for a week," Albigard pointed out. "I'm not certain you're qualified to speak on matters of safety."

"I get the sense we're not going to live this down anytime soon," Zorah put in. She sighed. "Len, be careful, okay? And give 'em hell."

"Perhaps not the *best* choice of idiom, love," Rans observed mildly. "Very well. We'll be off, as long as you're both certain about this. And... thank you for not giving up on us. Personally, I find the land of the living a much more attractive prospect than the land of the dead, these days." His gaze wandered to Zorah, an absent smile tilting one corner of his lips.

Rans recalled himself a moment later and shook Len's hand. Then he clasped Albigard forearm to forearm, like some ancient warriors' rite.

The Fae cleared his throat. "I am... gratified... that Nigellus was able to retrieve your souls," he said stiffly.

Rans smiled. "Ah, don't worry about it, Tinkerbell. You'll get over this unusual lapse soon enough. I'm confident we'll be hurling blades at each other again in no time."

Zorah caught Len's eye and mouthed '*homoerotic subtext*' at him from behind her raised hand. He choked on a snort and accepted her hug, followed by Vonnie's. Guthrie shook his hand with a firm, cool grip, and quietly said, "Thank you."

And just like that, they were leaving, with the cat-sidhe's promise to return soon so they could check in on the Court's progress later that afternoon. The front door closed, and the light from a Fae portal flared through the windows for a few moments before fading.

Silence settled over the little cottage, so complete that it echoed.

"How are you?" Len asked.

The Fae appeared mildly shell-shocked. "I have absolutely no idea."

"Right," Len said, squaring his shoulders. "When in doubt... food. Though we should probably take a miss on the mead for the moment."

"Eminently practical," Albigard replied, his tone sounding faint.

Len took a steadying breath, and went to explore the mysteries of the rustic little kitchen.

TWENTY-TWO

By the time he and Albigard had made inroads on another plowman's lunch of bread, cheese, fruit, and meat, the sidhe returned. The shape-shifter trotted into the room in animal form, and transformed without comment before plucking a slice of bread and some cheese from the remains of the platter.

"So, back to the Court, then?" Len asked, as the sidhe wolfed down the simple food with very little in the way of feline delicacy.

The diminutive Fae swallowed and nodded, brushing their fingers clean of crumbs and turning to Albigard. "I think so, yes. You'll be pleased to hear that all existing charges against you have been dropped, *a leanbh*. Apparently none of the surviving Court members cared to gamble on the Hunt's response to opposition in this matter." They shrugged. "I suppose it *would* be rather humiliating for the executioner to refuse to carry out the execution, and turn the axe on the jurors instead."

The news did nothing to improve Albigard's *system-rebooting-please-stand-by* expression, but Len breathed another internal sigh of relief. Making room for optimism was something he'd struggled with mightily over the years, for obvious reasons. However, at this rate, he might be in danger of thinking there was a happy ending in the works after all.

He gave the empty platter a quick wash and decided that the Court would just have to deal with his disheveled and unshowered state. Somehow, as a human, he doubted being primped and dressed to the nines would make much of a difference to the Fae's opinion of him.

Even so, he felt a moment of self-consciousness when the cat-sidhe gave a delicate sniff in his direction. A moment later, he understood.

The sidhe raised an eyebrow. "It is good that you found a use for your reserve of necromantic power, human. I trust Daeana not to bring trouble to your doorstep, but it might have been a bit much to parade you in front of the Court while you reeked of dead Fae. Not now, when there are likely to be fewer distractions than last time."

Len supposed that, when they'd shown up in the chamber yesterday, the presence of two-dozen armed Forsaken and the unleashed Hunt probably *had* been a bit higher on the Court's priority list than one human who stank of necromancy.

"Believe me," he said, "if we could avoid any more people dying for a bit, that would suit me right down to the ground."

"I cannot dispute the sentiment," Albigard agreed.

This Court session was much more sparsely attended than the last one Len had seen. The few spectators who'd braved the chamber were huddled at the farthest possible point in the room from the coiling darkness of the Hunt, which still stood vigil over the proceedings.

The sidhe strode down the aisle of the grand chamber without hesitation, as Len and Albigard followed close behind. "Magistrate," said the shape-shifter. "How fares the discussion regarding the Unseelie on Earth?"

The Magistrate drew breath to speak, only to be interrupted by a harried looking Court member from the Unseelie side.

"As a point of order, I have requested that the open seats on the Court be filled before such a major decision comes to a vote. As it stands now, there is an imbalance heavily favoring the Seelie contingent."

"And whose fault is that?" Len muttered, hopefully not loud enough for his words to reach the dais.

The Magistrate also appeared a bit frazzled— understandable, after recent events. "Indeed. Perhaps this interruption is a fortuitous one." She turned to Albigard. "Son of Oren, now that your name has been cleared and your honor restored, you are eligible to ascend to your father's seat on the Court."

Len's breath stuttered in his chest.

Albigard blinked at her in shock.

"*Never*," he said, with startling vehemence.

The Unseelie who'd been bitching about the open seats looked like he couldn't decide whether to be offended by the Magistrate's offer to someone who'd been a condemned criminal up until a few hours ago, or by the former condemned criminal turning his nose up at the offer.

"To ascend to the Fae Court is an *unparalleled honor—*" he began.

"I have no interest in counting myself among this body—one that can only seem to bring itself to do the right thing when the alternative is immediate death," Albigard said in low tones, cutting him off. "Do not speak to me of my father, or of *honor.* Certainly not in the same sentence."

Silence fell heavily over the chamber.

The cat-sidhe broke it, speaking in a wry tone. "I believe you have your answer."

Albigard sighed. "Give the seat to Teague," he said, sounding infinitely weary.

Len stared at him, not certain he'd heard correctly. "*What.*"

The Fae waved a hand. "At least one may be sure that his decisions will be in Dhuinne's interests, and not driven by sentiment."

The Magistrate tilted her head. "We will take the recommendation under advisement."

"And the Unseelie on Earth?" the cat-sidhe pressed.

"It is a complex issue that will require delicacy to deal with," said the Magistrate.

"Or you could just, y'know, *leave,*" Len suggested. "It's my world. Not yours. Your people being there is hurting both our realms. From where I'm standing, the solution seems pretty obvious."

Several of the Unseelie scoffed. The Magistrate gave Len a smooth politician's smile, though it seemed a bit strained around the edges.

"Unfortunately, it is not quite that simple," she said. "Would you prefer humanity to languish beneath the boot heel of our enemies, the demons?"

"At least there are only six hundred and sixty-six of them," Len said. "Not thousands. Also, the parties would probably be more fun."

"I believe you underestimate the degree to which human institutions rely on Fae support to function," the Magistrate replied with forced patience. "Stability on Earth has always been our goal. Not conquest."

Len stared at her. "And was stability the goal when you started killing off our world leaders, and tried to introduce a new ruling class of magical children at Stonehenge?" he asked. "Because if so— *news flash*—it didn't work."

A flush of pink colored the Magistrate's peaches and cream complexion. Meanwhile, the remaining Unseelie Court members suddenly seemed to find the various scrolls and parchments laid out in front of them intensely interesting.

"That was not an officially sanctioned course of action," the Magistrate informed Len coldly. "The perpetrators have been dealt with."

"My father and his supporters sanctioned that *course of action*," Albigard said in an acid tone. "And, as he was the head of the Unseelie Court at the time, the argument that it was not officially sanctioned appears facile at best."

The Magistrate didn't back down from his challenging gaze. "Your father is dead now. As are his supporters within the Court—including, I might add, one whom you yourself murdered last year. You have been offered a seat in Dhuinne's ruling body. With it, you might have influenced the Court from within. Instead, you turned it down. Nevertheless, perhaps all of us would be better served looking to the future, rather than the past."

The cat-sidhe had been watching the exchange closely. "As long as the future does not continue to repeat the same mistakes that brought us to this juncture in the first place," they said.

The Magistrate looked rather pointedly at the Wild Hunt, gathered in one corner of the chamber like a storm cloud. "There appears little danger of that." She visibly reined in her frustration, and continued. "I assure you, Elder—everyone here understands that action must be taken to correct the imbalance caused by the presence of the Unseelie on Earth. It remains only to decide what form that action will take, in order to cause the least amount of disruption... not only here, but also on Earth."

Len had the feeling that was about the best he could hope for, under the circumstances. The galling part was, she was probably right that yanking all ten thousand Unseelie back to Dhuinne without warning would finish the job of destabilizing human institutions that had already been severely stressed.

"Just... try to remember that humans deserve a say in their own futures, too?" he suggested. "It's not like we ever asked to be stuck in the middle of your feud with Hell."

The Magistrate's expression softened, if only for an instant. "That is a fair observation. And we are cognizant of your contribution to saving Dhuinne from ruin, Len Grayson of Earth. Your actions will not be forgotten."

After a bit more back and forth between the Magistrate and the cat-sidhe, they took their leave from the Court and returned to the cottage. Len wished he felt a bit more sanguine about what they'd truly accomplished.

"I will leave you for the night," said the sidhe. "I must visit the Forsaken and discuss their plans for liaising with the Court. You will be all right here until morning?"

"Yes, of course," Albigard said faintly.

He didn't sound all right, but the cat-sidhe only nodded and left them to it. Which was how Len found himself alone with a shell-shocked Fae and, presumably, several hours without any additional crises piling onto their heads.

"How are you doing after all of that?" Len asked, though of course he already knew the answer.

"Badly," Albigard said.

"Okay, same here," Len told him, aware that he should probably be fine right now, since Rans and Zorah were alive, and *he* wasn't the one who'd had to watch his father die the previous day.

In reality, Len just wanted to curl into a ball somewhere and rock for a bit. And while that wouldn't be terribly helpful to either of them, it did give him an idea. He barred the front door, figuring the cat-sidhe could just portal in when they returned. Then he threw some more food on a plate and grabbed the bottle of mead.

"Bedroom," he ordered. "The small one."

Albigard stood there blankly until Len nudged him with a shoulder, at which point he wandered toward the interior door in a daze. Len ushered him inside and set the food and drink on the little table.

"Stay here," he said. "I'll be right back, and then we're turning everything off... at least until tomorrow morning."

He made a second trip for a pitcher of water from the sink, along with a couple of clay cups. His third trip was to the other bedroom, and he returned with an armful of feather-stuffed pillows from the other beds. He dumped them on the floor in front of the bedside table, and piled the two pillows from this room's bed against the headboard on that side.

Throughout all of this, Albigard remained standing where Len had left him, hands hanging loosely at his sides. Lost.

Len uncorked the mead and took a couple of deep swallows—just enough to send a flush of heady warmth radiating outward from his stomach to his arms and legs. Then he handed the bottle to Albigard.

"Drink enough of that to take the edge off," he ordered. "When you're done, take your boots off and get comfortable."

He demonstrated by kicking off his Doc Martens, peeling off his socks, and shrugging out of the commandant vest with its aggressive military-style metal bars on the shoulders. The he flopped onto the bed, naked to the waist, sitting against the pillows at the headboard with one leg draped over the mattress edge and the other stretched out in front of him.

"You stink," Albigard observed neutrally, holding the bottle loosely in his hand as though he'd forgotten about it already.

"Yeah, sorry about that," Len said. "There's no shower in this place."

Albigard's brow furrowed, and he made an intricate gesture with his free hand. Len swallowed a yelp of surprise as a sharp tingle rushed over his body from head to toe. When it faded, the smell of stale sweat and body odor had disappeared, along with the unpleasant sensation of greasy hair and grimy skin. In fact, he felt kind of like he'd just been sandblasted with exfoliant.

"Okay," he said slowly. "That's... handy. Um, thanks. Now hurry up and get mildly drunk—you look miserable and it's upsetting me."

The Fae gave him an odd look, but he raised the bottle to his lips and started chugging. Len wouldn't have pegged him as a guzzler—not with that tight-laced demeanor and air of tragic nobility. Which only went to show that you should never make assumptions about people, he supposed.

When the bottle was empty, Albigard set it on the table and toed off his tall boots. Len let him decide for himself what constituted 'getting comfortable,' and was pleased when he unlaced the stiff brocade tunic and slid out of it. Clad only in his loose-sleeved linen undershirt and soft leather breeches, he lowered himself gracefully onto the nest of pillows by the bed without being told. After a moment's hesitation, he let his head fall to rest against Len's thigh.

Len's heart gave an awkward double-thud as he reached out a hand and stroked fingers over gossamer hair. "There you go, princeling," he said softly. "We're going to stay like this for a bit. When we get hungry later, we'll eat. When the sun goes down, we'll sleep. And that's all. You don't have to worry about anything else tonight."

Albigard gave a small, silent nod of agreement against Len's leg. Len let all his pesky thoughts drain away with a sense of palpable relief, leaving his mind pleasantly empty except for the warm weight of Albigard's head against his thigh and the soft strands of hair beneath his fingers. He traced the braids running along the Fae's temple and began to unravel them with slow strokes, until the blond mane was loose and flowing free.

For a long time, Albigard stayed silent and quiescent beneath the gentle petting. Eventually, he shifted in place.

"I am *not* my father," he said. It was barely a whisper, for all its vehemence.

Len paused in running his fingers through the Fae's silky hair, then resumed his rhythmic stroking a few moments later.

"I know you're not," he said quietly.

TWENTY-THREE

The morning sun streaming through the round bedroom window illuminated the pale hair draped over Len's bare chest like a silvery halo. He yawned and blinked, thinking that he could get used to waking up like this... even if his left arm was completely numb after being slept on all night.

Albigard's head rested heavy and warm on his shoulder. One arm and one leg splayed possessively across Len's body. As far as he could tell, nothing appeared to be trying to kill them. Or arrest them. Or relay dire warnings to them about the end of the world being imminent.

It was nice.

Len's dick began to sit up and take notice of *exactly* how nice it was. He stretched, luxuriating in the feeling of Albigard's body shifting against his... and that was when he noticed the black cat sitting primly on the bedside table, its tail curled around its toes as it stared at him.

"*Damn it,*" he said, scrambling for the sheets in instinctive embarrassment—only to remember that they were both still wearing clothes from the waist down, and anyway the sheets were already pulled modestly over his and Albigard's hips. He let his head flop back against the pillow as Albigard blinked awake.

"What is it?" the Fae murmured, in the resigned tone of someone who wouldn't have been remotely surprised to find aliens invading or Godzilla laying waste to the city... but was still *so* done with it all.

"Visitor," Len told him, and jerked his chin toward the cat-sidhe.

"Oh," Albigard said.

The cat jumped down to the floor and morphed into humanoid form. "Good morning. Do you always sleep so *late*? Aesulna is here. She wishes to speak with you."

Albigard rolled onto an elbow, and Len could almost see him restacking all of his worries into place after last night's brief respite. "Very well. A few moments to make ourselves presentable, please."

The sidhe snorted. "I doubt a Forsaken will be offended by your bare feet, *a leanbh*. But I will pass on the message."

With that, they left.

"Well," Len mused, "it was nice while it lasted, I guess."

"It was... restful," Albigard agreed. He rose from the bed and stretched, drawing Len's gaze to the taut, graceful lines of his body.

Down, boy, Len told his dick sternly, as the Fae went looking for the rest of his clothing. A moment later, he caught the vest Albigard tossed at him and slid it on, zipping up the front and fastening the decorative buckles. His clothing was definitely beginning to look the worse for wear after so many days spent roughing it in the Fae realm, but there wasn't a lot he could do about it. After pulling on his Docs and running his fingers through his fringe of hair, he exchanged a look with his companion.

"Any idea what this is about?" he asked.

"None," Albigard replied. "Hopefully nothing catastrophic, or I assume the sidhe would have woken us sooner."

"*Cat*-astrophic," Len echoed with flat humor. "*Ha*. Good one."

The Fae leveled a severe look in his direction and headed for the front room. Len tagged along behind.

Aesulna was waiting for them, seated on a chair and sipping steaming tea from a cup.

"Good morning, friends," she said placidly.

"Good morning, Aesulna," Albigard replied, with more courtesy than Len could ever remember hearing from him before. "Is everything well?"

Aesulna smiled. "If that's a polite way of asking if any new crises are looming, the answer is no. Not to my knowledge, at any rate. In fact, I am here with a proposal for you, Albigard of the Unseelie."

Albigard raised a curious eyebrow. "Are you indeed?"

"The camp has been discussing the Court's offer of liaison," she went on. "We have chosen our representatives to this proposed *committee*." The word was laced with both amusement and contempt. "All except for one. You do not belong here in the city, Albigard. And yet, you understand the Court and its minions better than those of us who fled to the wildlands to escape the rules of Fae society. You speak their language, but you would fight

for *our* freedoms. We wish you to be our final rep-
resentative, bridging the gap between the Forsaken
and the Court."

Len watched the look of shock flit across Albigard's face for an instant before he covered it.

"I… would need to consider the offer," said
the Fae.

Aesulna tipped her head. "Understandable.
And to be clear, whether you accept it or not, you
will always have a place in our camp should you
desire it." She set her tea down and rose. "Inform
us of your decision whenever you are ready, if you
would. You know where to find us."

With a kind smile that also included Len, she
dipped her chin in farewell and left the cottage.

The cat-sidhe gave Albigard and Len a brief
onceover, and rose as well. "Well, now. It appears
you have some things to consider. I will be in the
other bedroom when you've come to a decision regarding your course of action."

Like a piano falling on him out of the blue, it
hit Len that there was now a future to think about.
And yes, that sounded stupid even in his own
head—but in his defense, up until very recently
he'd been working on the assumption that the
world was going to end and they were all going to
die. His brain hadn't quite flipped the switch yet, it
seemed.

Because they *hadn't* died, and it looked like the
world was maybe, probably, hopefully not going to
end after all… and he'd been playing house in a
parallel dimension with someone who wasn't even
the same species as he was. Someone who had a

life — and a lifespan — that Len could barely conceive of, while Len had friends and a house and a job back on Earth.

The realization felt like a bucket of ice water to the face.

"That would" — he broke off and cleared his throat when the words stumbled — "That, uh, sounds like something you'd be really good at."

Albigard was still staring at the front door after Aesulna's exit. "I..." He hesitated. "Perhaps."

"Did you have other plans?" To be honest, Len had no idea what sort of life Albigard usually lived when he wasn't busy pissing off his own people and almost getting executed.

"In truth?" said the Fae. "I hadn't expected to survive this long."

Evidently, the Fae had been smacked upside the head by the same clue-by-four that had just walloped Len. He wasn't sure if that made things better or worse.

"Yeah? Same here." Len strove to keep his tone light. "You made it, though. Saved the world, got your criminal record expunged, and now the Court owes you big time. You've just gotta keep an eye on them to make sure they take care of the Unseelie problem on Earth, and other than that, you can do whatever you want now, right?"

Albigard honestly looked as though the idea hadn't occurred to him until this very moment. "I... suppose so." His green gaze met Len's and held. "And you? What will you do now?"

Len took a deep breath. "I mean...? Go back to Earth and try to avoid being near anyone or anything that's dying, I guess?"

The Fae's brow furrowed. "Yes." He almost sounded like he was speaking to himself. "Even with the Court's good graces, I suppose it would be dangerous here, for anyone with necromancy."

"Well," Len said, "Like I said, I've already got a life on Earth, too. Maybe it's not the greatest life, but it includes some people I care about."

"You have roots in the human realm," Albigard murmured. "Of course you do."

Len thought about Kat... about Maurice and Sally, and the other employees at the Brown Fox. About Guthrie and Vonnie... Rans and Zorah.

Roots.

"I do, yes." He swallowed. "And the last thing you need here is some kind of diplomatic incident caused by a human necromancer, right? I can't even seem to control it properly... and in all honesty, I don't really *want* to control that kind of power."

Albigard nodded slowly. "I understand that now. I see that it wasn't something you asked for, or wanted—even if I have cause to be grateful for your unwanted abilities on a... personal level."

This was quickly turning into one of the most awkward conversations of Len's life. There was simply no opening where it would be appropriate to say *I've seen you fall apart in my arms*, or *I felt you die while I was kissing you*.

He was standing in front of someone who'd witnessed the fall of the Holy Roman Empire, and all Len could think about was the desperate light behind Albigard's forest-green eyes right before he lost control and begged for sexual release.

It occurred to him belatedly that these past few weeks had been... some kind of fever dream. A time outside of time, when the rules no longer applied because everything was going to hell in a handbasket and none of it mattered anyway. But now it was over.

They'd survived. They'd even *won*.

And things would go back to normal.

Mouth dry, Len said, "So. I guess that's it, huh?"

Albigard was watching him very intently. "You wish to return to the human realm."

It hadn't really been phrased as a question.

"I mean... if there's nothing more I can do to help here, I guess I probably should," Len managed. And it was true—he needed to check in with the others. Let Kat know he was okay. Make sure he still had a job.

The Fae nodded. "Very well."

The simple acceptance made Len's stomach turn over. But what other response was he expecting?

"Will you take Aesulna up on her offer, do you think?" he asked, mostly to have something to say.

He liked the idea of Albigard being among other Fae who accepted him—who *valued* him—for exactly who and what he was. Len could picture him deep in conversation about magical theory with Leesa, or planning political strategy with Nezri and Danon. It made him feel better to believe

that the prickly bastard wouldn't end up alone, because the Forsaken wouldn't *let* him be alone.

"I will have to think on it," Albigard said. "But
perhaps you are right that it would... suit me."

"I really believe it would," Len said past the
growing lump in his throat. "If nothing else, I
imagine Oren would be absolutely livid about the
idea, if he were alive to see."

"Very true," Albigard agreed. "Very, *very*
true."

Silence stretched painfully.

"Right." Len cleared his throat. "So... I guess I
should probably talk to the cat-sidhe now. I imagine they can get me through the gateway without
pissing off the guards any more than we already
have. And maybe they'll give me a ride back to St.
Louis, since I don't have a passport. Or money, for
that matter."

It seemed wrong to blurt out his intention to
leave right away so casually, but at this moment,
Len felt utterly incapable of addressing anything
more personal. Not without immediately descending into stammering idiocy, anyway. He started to
turn away — to head for the bedroom door and let
the cat-sidhe know he needed to go back to Earth —
but a callused hand touched his jaw, stopping him.

Len's breath caught, and he had to force himself to meet Albigard's eyes without flinching.

"You have my everlasting gratitude, for everything you have done," said the Fae. "For me. For
my people. For my home. I will not forget it."

"Don't mention it," Len whispered hoarsely,
and fled.

TWENTY-FOUR

A week later, Len lay on his couch, staring at the ceiling of his borrowed nineteen forties two-bedroom bungalow and wondering what the ever-loving *fuck* he'd been thinking.

The cat-sidhe had ushered him through the gateway to Earth, dragged him along the ley lines to North America, and portaled him back to his neighborhood. When he'd tried to thank them for all of their help, the sidhe had given him a pleasant smile, followed by an expression that looked suspiciously like pity.

Sometimes it is necessary to make mistakes before growth may occur, they'd said — rather cryptically, in Len's opinion. After which, the little Fae had turned into a cat and trotted away, leaving Len alone on the street corner where the Wild Hunt had first tried to rip its way into the human realm.

He'd stood there, blinking — surrounded by tender shoots of green grass poking through the straw mulch covering the surrounding yards. Late summer was giving way to the brisk breeziness of early autumn. Len had oriented himself and walked the couple of blocks back to Zorah's house, where he let himself in through the patio door and collapsed on the creaking couch, his mind whirling.

The first day after his return, he'd dragged out his aging laptop to check his bank account balance, because he currently had no vehicle, no groceries to speak of, and no cell phone. Then he'd gone into the bathroom and splashed cold water on his face before checking it again, because the balance was fifty thousand dollars higher than it should have been.

The online entry was still there the second time he looked—*BANK OF MALDIVES PLC PMT IAT $50,000*, dated the previous day. At that point, he'd started cursing creatively.

When he'd finished cursing, he'd checked the city bus schedule, dragged his 'emergency cash' envelope out of the slit in the upholstery at the back of the couch, stuffed four hundred dollars in his pocket, then headed out to buy a cheap phone and some food.

Once he'd taken care of those two important errands, he checked the city's website to find out what it was going to cost to get Rans' motorcycle out of the impound lot, after he'd left it illegally parked on the Delmar Loop. When he had the relevant info, he emailed it directly to the vampire rather than dealing with it himself—since Len didn't actually own the bike, while Rans could easily stroll in and mesmerize the staff to get his beloved Triumph back.

Sorry I ditched your motorcycle, Bela, he added at the end of the message. *World at stake, lives hanging in the balance, etc., etc. Also, did you deposit $50K in my bank account? Because if so, take it back.*

The reply came an hour later.

As long as the Triumph is in one piece, you're forgiven under the circumstances. And no, it wasn't me. I don't even know which bank you use, mate. Oh, and Zorah says welcome back to Earth. Did Alby come here with you?

Len hadn't emailed him back.

The following day, he'd sent a message to Gina, because if the Brown Fox was open again, he figured he should probably find out if he still had a job or not. He tried not to focus on how hard he was finding it to care one way or the other, while still reeling from the events of the past few weeks.

Hello, Len, came the reply. *I understand you've been dealing with some rather extraordinary issues since the club reopened. Sally tells me she's had Manuel running the kitchen in your absence, so talk to her about getting you back on the schedule. Everyone has missed you. Welcome home. Gina.*

He'd closed his eyes after reading the message. Manuel was twenty-three, a terrific cook, and had a sick mother to support. The promotion to Len's old position would be life changing for him. He'd also be great at the job.

Len didn't reply to that email, either.

More time passed. He started taking really long walks in an attempt to shut his brain off, trekking along the streets that had been sucked dry by the Wild Hunt. The neighborhood was slowly reemerging, as the grass grew and new families moved in. While he walked, he kept an eye out for any familiar faces — any hint that someone besides him had survived the destruction. There were none, but then again, he'd only known a couple of dozen people on his immediate street to say hello to.

On one morning's walk, he'd jolted out of a half-aware state to discover that his aching feet had carried him all the way to Carondelet Park. He was standing in the middle of the sidewalk, staring at a freshly installed telephone pole. But in his mind it was broken, with a smoking wreck of a car wrapped around it. His hands were shaking as he walked back to the house.

Several times during the week, Len reminded himself that he needed to call Kat and let her know he was all right. Each time, the prospect of pretending that everything was fine defeated him, and he told himself he'd do it the following day.

On Sunday afternoon, a determined knock sounded at the front door.

Sprawled on the rickety couch, Len stared at a cobweb on the ceiling and debated ignoring it. The knock came again, louder this time. It sounded like the knock of someone who wasn't going away anytime soon. He rose reluctantly, the stiffness of his joints making him wonder just how long he'd been lying there. His spine creaked and popped as he stretched.

A fresh flurry of pounding sounded just as he reached the front door, and he opened it with a certain sense of inevitability. Kat stood framed in the opening, with Gabe standing behind her, hanging back a couple of paces.

"What the *hell*, Len?" she demanded, fist still poised in the air, mid-knock.

"Hi, Kat," he said. "Sorry… it's, um, not really a good time…"

Kat stared at him for a beat, before putting a hand in the middle of his chest and pushing him backward a couple of steps so she could walk past him.

"Invite Gabe in," she ordered. "He's too polite to barge."

"Er… come in?" Len managed, submitting to the steamrolling because there was no denying he really *should* have called her before now.

"Thanks," Gabe murmured, and slipped in so Len could close the door after him.

Kat frog-marched Len to the sofa and pushed him down on it before sitting next to him. She didn't even flinch at the furniture's piteous groan of protest. Gabe hovered. Len considered offering him a chair, but was cut off before he could get the words out.

"I had to learn you were back from Sally, you idiot!" Kat said. "From *Sally*! Tell me — what's wrong with this picture?"

"I'm sorry, Kat —" he began.

She wasn't done yet.

"Don't you 'sorry' me, Len Grayson! The last time we spoke, people around you were dying and you looked like you were one crisis away from a breakdown! Now you're back here, hiding out in your house and not answering calls or emails. So *start talking.*"

"I lost my phone," he said, and knew immediately that the ridiculous evasion had been a mistake. Kat puffed up as if she was about to explode, and he hurried on. "Really, I *am* sorry... it's been completely crazy for weeks now, and I'm not really, uh, dealing with it very well."

The threat of imminent explosion receded visibly.

"So you thought you'd cut yourself off from your friends?" she prodded. "How's that working out for you?"

Len sagged, propping his elbows on his knees and putting his face in his hands.

"About as well as you might expect," he said. "Gabe... apologies, man. Grab a chair or something. There's drinks in the fridge if you want one."

"Thanks," Gabe replied. "Assuming you really want me here, I mean. I can give you two some privacy if you'd rather."

Len remembered the way Gabe had looked at Kat when he'd warned them to keep each other safe. His throat tightened.

"No," he said, looking up. "You're fine. Make yourself at home and get ready to suspend your disbelief."

Once Gabe was settled, Len took a deep breath and started talking. It was surprisingly difficult to start, and surprisingly hard to stop once he got going. He detailed Albigard's abduction after the car chase that destroyed the pimpmobile, their escape to the pocket realm, the fact that his erstwhile ghosts were actually necromantic animus, and how that animus had powered their travel back to Earth with the Wild Hunt hot on their heels.

He told them about Albigard's insistence on returning to the Fae realm, and their rescue by the

Forsaken. He explained about the world tree, and the horrible moment when the Hunt had killed Albigard and nearly escaped Chaima's grasp. He recounted Albigard's unlikely resurrection, and the Hunt's reappearance. He talked about confronting the Fae Court, Nigellus retrieving Rans and Zorah's souls, and the sudden realization that they'd made it... that the crisis was over and they'd survived.

While he didn't share the gritty details, he also didn't gloss over the fact that he'd fallen for — and fallen into bed with — a centuries-old Fae who lived in a different dimension. Someone with whom he couldn't possibly have a future. He finished with the horrifically awkward conversation in which they'd both realized that fact at roughly the same time, and Len had slunk back to Earth before it occurred to him that he had no freaking clue what to do with the rest of his life.

"Oh, *sweetheart*," Kat said, once he'd wound down like a broken toy. "What were you *thinking*?"

"I don't know," he said, a bit desperately. "Kat, I don't *know*. It's crazy. It could never work. I mean... that's what I was thinking, I guess?" He buried his face in his hands. "Jesus. This is *whacked*. He probably hasn't given it a single thought since I left."

"You mean the same guy who glared holes through my skull for hugging you? Bet you a dollar he has," Kat said dryly.

Len squeezed the bridge of his nose. "And if he has? So what? I'm still human, and he's still Fae. Nothing's changed. This isn't some fairy tale romance with a guaranteed happy ending."

Gabe—who'd listened silently to the whole sorry retelling—shot him a wry look. "A *fairy* tale romance? I think you'll find it is, by its very definition."

Len groaned and started laughing, because that was better than the alternative. "Okay, now I see why Kat fell for you," he managed, once he'd regained control.

"Seriously, though," Gabe went on. "Did you talk about this with him *at all* before you hightailed it back to Earth?"

"Of course he didn't," Kat answered for him, saving him the trouble.

"So... maybe try doing that?" Gabe said.

"Right?" Kat agreed. "I mean, there's got to be someone who can get a message to him. Maybe the vampires? They owe you big time, after all."

Len stamped on a little bubble of feeling in his chest that was probably hope. "What would that even look like, though? I mentioned the part about different dimensions, didn't I?"

Gabe frowned. "But for these guys, it's just... *poof.* And you're in a different world, or hurtling across the ocean through a magic portal and stepping out in St. Louis an instant later. So if you don't want to live there permanently, commute."

Len opened his mouth to explain why that couldn't possibly work, thought about it for a minute, and closed his mouth.

"I have no idea if that's even something he'd want," he said instead.

Kat didn't roll her eyes at him, but it looked like a close-run thing. "So ask him."

"In that much of a hurry to be rid of me?" Len asked. "Now I see how it is."

She held his gaze, not letting him get away with trying to lighten the mood. "I just want you to be happy, you lump. And you're miserable right now. So *do something different*, already."

Len tried to picture what *happy* looked like. It was surprisingly difficult. He'd managed *content* at times. He'd occasionally even graduated to *fulfilled* for brief periods—usually when he was running a kitchen and feeding people.

He flashed back to a lazy morning awakening with a blond head resting on his shoulder, sunlight haloing the sleeping body tangled with his.

"Shit," he whispered.

Kat raised an eyebrow. "Is that code for '*yes, Kat, I'll do exactly what you and your awesome boyfriend suggest*'?"

"Yes, Kat, I'll do exactly what you and your awesome boyfriend suggest," Len replied meekly.

Kat leaned over and enveloped him in a squishy, all-encompassing hug. "Good answer, babe. Now, promise to keep me informed of how it goes, and let me know whenever you're in town so we can get together and dish gossip."

"I promise," he said, and let himself be squished.

The pair left soon after. Len watched out the window as Gabe opened the passenger door of his SUV for Kat before letting himself into the driver's side. The engine roared to life a moment later, and they drove away.

He stared after them for a bit longer, trying to gather his thoughts. Opening his laptop, he took a deep breath and tackled the backlog of emails he'd been ignoring. To Rans and Zorah — *Sorry, I've been wallowing in my bad decision-making skills for the last few days. No, Albigard didn't come back with me. In fact, that's wrapped up with the previously mentioned bad decision-making, and now I need to get in touch with him so we can talk. Do you have a way to reach him?*

To Sally — *I apologize for not getting in touch with you re: scheduling at the Brown Fox. That was really unprofessional. The truth is, Manuel needs that position more than I do. It's also possible that I'll be traveling back and forth to the Fae realm of Dhuinne quite a bit in the future. But if this plan blows up in my face (probably not literally this time ha ha), I would be immensely grateful for a job tending bar the next time there's an opening.*

He also emailed Vonnie with a much more concise version of the *'help, I've fallen for a Fae'* speech he'd just poured out to Kat, because A) she deserved to know, and B) she could probably sympathize with an unexpected romantic attachment to a supernatural creature.

When he was done, he took a shower, made himself a decent meal, and watched TV for a few hours before checking for replies to his messages. Sally wouldn't see the work email until tomorrow. There was no reply yet from Rans. Vonnie, however, had sent him a supportive note that included the phrase *'go get him, tiger'* in an apparently non-ironic way. She also apologized and informed him that neither she nor Guthrie had a way to reach Albigard while he was in Dhuinne.

Figuring Rans would be a better bet on that front, he went to bed. If nothing else, Rans almost certainly knew how to reach Nigellus, and Len was willing to bet Nigellus had a way to contact the cat-sidhe. The faintly pitying look the sidhe had given Len when they parted was starting to make a lot more sense now, as embarrassing as that was to admit.

Whatever the case, he'd done what he could for today. The fact that he'd finally pulled his head out of his ass — or rather, that Kat had pulled his head out of his ass for him — did wonders to combat his black depression. He fell asleep in only a few minutes, and was out like a light.

He blinked awake the following morning to find the sun stabbing his eyeballs through the bedroom window, and the sound of an impossibly familiar eight-cylinder engine rumbling in the driveway.

TWENTY-FIVE

The pimpmobile was parked in Len's driveway. Which... wasn't right. He opened the front door, only vaguely aware that he was wearing pajama bottoms and nothing else.

"What?" he said to the empty air, as his just-woken brain tried to reconcile the shiny paintjob and lack of rust with the almost-but-not-quite familiar pattern of bullet holes in the quarter panel of the 1978 Lincoln Continental.

Then, the driver's door opened, and a blond figure stepped out.

"Seriously... *what*?" Len asked, with a bit more feeling behind it this time.

"I replaced your car," Albigard said, walking up to the concrete steps leading to the porch. "Even though it was not a very good car."

"You... replaced my car," Len echoed stupidly.

Albigard's brow furrowed. "It seemed important to you." He cleared his throat and continued, "I'm afraid the body shop was unable to replicate the pattern of rust. They also refused to replicate the bullet holes, so I had to do those myself. I trust my memory of the pattern was accurate."

Len stared at him. Then he sat down rather abruptly on the top step and started to laugh. Even to his own ears, it sounded pretty far on the wrong side of hysterical.

The Fae peered at him quizzically. "Are you... well?"

Len got himself under control with difficulty. "Did you deposit fifty thousand dollars in my bank account last week?" he asked.

"No," Albigard said. "That sounds like something one of the bloodsuckers would do."

Something in Len's chest unknotted. "Well, it wasn't Rans." he paused then, as realization struck. "Oh. It was probably Guthrie. He has access to my banking information from when I worked for him. Right."

"For what it's worth, I'd imagine he can afford it," Albigard offered. "And you *did* help to save his granddaughter's soul from the Endless Void."

Len waved the words away. "I'll tell him to take it back next time I talk to him. Never mind." He hauled himself to his feet and descended until he was standing on the lowest step, face to face with the Fae. Something seemed... different about him, and it took Len a moment to realize he was back in his *'don't mind me, I'm just a normal human'* guise, with his faunlike ears and gracefully swept eyebrows glamoured to be round and boring. "You didn't have to replace the pimpmobile, you know," he added.

Albigard shrugged. "No. I did not have to. But it seemed like the correct thing to do. Is the vehicle acceptable?"

With a deep breath, Len forced himself to ignore the Fae's magnetic pull. He walked barefoot and shirtless to the driveway, where he did a full three-sixty around the shiny Lincoln, trailing his fingertips over the flawless paintjob.

"I love it," he said, brushing a thumb over the topmost bullet hole... which was situated a bit too far to the left. "Thank you."

"You are most welcome." Albigard drew breath to say more, but hesitated uncharacteristically.

"What is it?" Len asked.

The Fae raised his chin. "I have... a proposal, I suppose you might say. I know Dhuinne holds danger for you as a necromancer, even now. However, I have been spending more time among the Forsaken since we parted. They do not fear your powers. Indeed, Leesa asks after you often. I thought... perhaps..."

"The answer is yes," Len told him, not even stopping to think about it.

Albigard frowned. "You do not know what I was going to ask."

"Yes, I'll come with you to Dhuinne, with the understanding that I do also have a life on Earth, and will want to come back here periodically," Len clarified. "Anyway, you already knew that, or you wouldn't have bothered with the car."

"Oh," Albigard said.

"Do you have to go back right away? It'll take me a few days to arrange everything and let my friends know what's going on."

"I will need to travel to Dhuinne for a meeting of the new liaison committee tomorrow, but returning here afterward will not be a problem."

Len raised an eyebrow. "You ended up taking the job, then."

One corner of Albigard's lips turned up. "I did, yes. I was informed by someone who knew me well that it would suit me."

"And does it?" Len asked, feeling fairly confident of the answer.

"So far, certainly."

An answering smile tugged at Len's mouth. "Come inside," he said. "I'll make breakfast. Not Pop-Tarts, I promise."

Albigard's green eyes shone. "That sounds... most agreeable."

Len led him into the house, his chest feeling as light as air.

EPILOGUE

The sounds of daily life in the camp of the Forsaken formed a comforting background murmur, as Len hovered over a steaming cauldron near the back of the cave. He ladled a small amount of stew into the bowl he was holding and handed it to Leesa, who blew on it for a moment before taking a sip.

"It's good," she said. "The salt tastes right, but I think it would be better with more ground tsainabark. It's a bit bland right now."

"We can do that," Len agreed, and went rummaging through the collection of clay containers on the shelf near the cooking fire. Leesa smirked and shook her head when he picked up the first jar and showed it to her, but nodded in confirmation at his second guess.

"You're starting to get it, I think," she teased.

"Well, if you insist on labeling the containers in an alphabet I can't read," he shot back.

"I could teach you," Leesa said with a smile. "If you're going to spend time here, you should at least know how to read and write." A frown wrinkled her smooth brow, and she ruffled a hand through her freshly dyed blue hair. It matched Len's, after he'd brought along a box of his preferred brand and showed her how to use it. "I don't know if you can learn to speak properly, though," she continued. "I'm not sure how to do it since Dhuinne is already translating for you."

"I think my best bet on that front is to stay on Dhuinne's good side," he told her.

She snickered. "I'd say so, yes."

Len added more of the powdery brown seasoning to the cauldron, which was large enough to feed the entire camp. This time, Leesa made an impressed face after tasting it. "Now *that's* good."

Len tried a bit as well. He still found it difficult to judge nuance, since all Fae food tasted amazing to his run-of-the-mill human palate. The flavor profile seemed decent, though, with a hint of spicy heat and a rich depth of umami.

"If you're happy, I'm happy," he said, and swung the cauldron away from the fire to cool for a bit.

Leesa's answering smile was brilliant. "You really are, aren't you? I'm glad you came back."

The airy lightness that spilled through Len's chest at random moments still had the capacity to take him by surprise. He breathed through it for a few seconds before he could trust his voice.

"So am I," he said.

A small commotion arose outside the cave. "They're back!" someone called.

Len's attention moved to the cave entrance as though drawn by a magnet, and a few moments later he was rewarded by the entrance of a small group with Albigard at its center.

Albigard's gaze swept the cavern until it came to rest on Len, and their eyes locked. The little swoop in Len's stomach would never get old; nor would the softening of Albigard's expression whenever Len caught the Fae looking at him.

Several members of the camp approached the group, asking questions and dispensing the day's news. The twins fielded most of the chatter, until Danon boomed, "Food first. Then talk. We've got news as well, but we might as well share it with everyone at once, rather than piecemeal."

"Stew's ready!" Leesa piped up from her position at Len's side. "Bring your bowls and let's eat!"

The Forsaken didn't need to be told twice, and soon the two of them were ladling out portions to a line of hungry camp members. Albigard appeared at Len's shoulder, his braided hair gleaming in the firelight.

"Cutting the line?" Len asked. "For shame."

Albigard raised a tolerant eyebrow. "Nonsense. I wouldn't dare." He paused while Len served up another portion, then continued. "The Court has come to a decision on the matter of the Unseelie on Earth at last," he said. "You will not like it. However, I believe it does represent a step forward, at the very least."

Len sighed. The Court had been dragging its feet on the issue. That fact alone had been something of a red flag. "Do I need to go yell at them some more? Not that it's likely to make much more of an impact than it did last time."

"In due course, perhaps," Albigard allowed. "For now, I think it would be best to allow the current changes time to settle. As I said, it is still progress of an incremental sort."

Len got the last few people served, and went to find a comfortable spot to sit. Albigard lowered himself to sit next to him, content to leave the speaking to the twins and Aesulna.

After a rundown of the day's business in the new committee, Nezri met Len's eyes. "While it is not Forsaken business directly, the Court has finally ruled on the Unseelie presence in the human realm. In order to rebalance Dhuinne's magic, they have decreed that half of the Unseelie wardens on Earth will be recalled, and replaced with Seelie. The Seelie will take over their duties to prevent what they call *unnecessary disruption*."

Len's heart sank.

"In the current climate," Albigard murmured in his ear, "I would place more trust in Seelie wardens to rule from behind the scenes with empathy and thoughtfulness."

So would Len, but that didn't mean he was happy about the prospect of continued Fae control of Earth.

"It is what it is," he managed. "Like you said, baby steps." At least it would probably succeed in fixing Dhuinne's magic. Already, the imbalance was improving after the Wild Hunt had been absorbed into Chaima. Life had returned quickly to the area around the Forsaken camp, but the vines no longer made a daily all-out assault on the cave entrance and walking paths. Presumably, these additional changes would finally return things to whatever constituted normal in a world inhabited by magical faeries.

He shook off the political setback with a determined air, and gave Albigard a thorough onceover. "You look beat," he observed.

Albigard raised one shoulder in a careless shrug. "Not fatigued, so much as tired of listening to politicians prattle endlessly. I suppose it comes with the job."

Len smiled at him. "Maybe it does... when you're in the city," he said, and lifted a hand to cup the Fae's chin, brushing a thumb across his lower lip before letting him go. "But here, your role is entirely different. Or had you forgotten, princeling?"

Albigard's eyes darkened in the flickering light. "How could I forget, with you to remind me?"

"Mmm," Len agreed. "Give me a few hours to set some things up. Come find me by the hot springs... erm, what time does the moon rise tonight?"

"About an hour before midnight," Albigard replied.

"Come find me when the moon rises, then." Len finished his stew, and left the Fae to wonder what, exactly, he was in for.

⸻ ◆ ⸻

Hours later, when Albigard entered the grotto housing the hot springs, Len was waiting for him on a pile of furs and blankets that he'd dragged down from the collection kept on the carved stone shelf at the top of the trail. He'd taken off his shirt—mostly because it was hot next to the steaming pools—but was still wearing his jeans, along with the thong necklace Leesa had made for him, with Albigard's faded cotton hair tie braided into the weave.

Nearby lay coils of rope, a knife sharp enough to cut that rope, a clay jar of oil, and a rubber ball attached to a leather strap that he'd tossed into his bag on a whim when he'd been packing to leave for Dhuinne.

A few other Fae were lounging in the pools, including one pair who were clearly having sex— the woman straddling her partner's lap beneath the water as they rocked together. Len had spoken quietly to several people over the course of the evening, ensuring that he wasn't about to shatter any unspoken Forsaken taboos. He'd come away further reassured that no one here cared how or with whom you had sex, as long as everyone involved was adult and there of their own free will.

Furthermore, they were well aware that some of their members preferred the illusion of non-consent—not a real shock given the kind of screwed-up psychological warfare that mainstream Fae society foisted on their queer children and adolescents. Bottom line, the Forsaken were cool with kinks like Albigard's, as long as no one got hurt or emotionally traumatized. Len was relieved to discover this... not to mention a little bit intrigued by the possibilities it opened up. Indeed, he intended to play with those possibilities to some small extent tonight, assuming Albigard consented.

The Fae in question approached Len cautiously. "The moon is up; I am here, as summoned."

Len smiled up at him, not rising. "And wearing far too many clothes. Strip, please."

Albigard lifted his chin, playing at defiance.

Len gestured at the little dagger lying nearby. "Or, I mean, I could always tie you up first and cut them off you. It seems wasteful, though."

The Fae gave him the barest hint of an eye-roll, and Len had to hide a smile. He did start stripping efficiently, though — mission accomplished. When he was bare, his pale hair hanging free and his tattoos twisting in the flickering light cast by the hundreds of sprites that inhabited the grotto, Len pointed to the edge of the furs on which he was reclining.

"Kneel there," he said. "We need to have one of those discussions you don't see the point of."

"Witness my surprise," Albigard replied in a dry tone, even as he lowered himself gracefully to his knees where Len had indicated.

"Cheeky," Len retorted. "Anyway, real talk. If you agree to it, some people might show up tonight while you're nominally helpless, and interact with us. I'll be the only one to physically touch you, though — even if they imply other people might. Does that appeal at all?"

Albigard's brows drew together. "This place continues to surprise me day after day."

"Not really an answer, princeling," Len pointed out.

The Fae took a deep breath. "I find the idea both intriguing and disquieting. But I believe the intrigue outweighs the disquiet."

"Fair enough," Len told him. "The moment that changes, signal me and I'll make them go away. That's always the deal, as you hopefully know by now."

The faintest hint of amusement washed across Albigard's features. "You do seem insistent on driving the point home repeatedly."

"What can I say? It's how I roll," Len said. "Which leads to the next point. Can you cast a ball of illumination even if you're distracted, or restrained? Or both?"

"Yes," the Fae replied.

Len nodded. "All right. Tonight, that's your signal if you can't speak to say yellow or red. One sparkly magic ball for 'slow down,' two sparkly magic balls for 'stop.' Will that work?"

Albigard still looked faintly amused. "As well as anything."

"And it's preferable to you simply blasting me off my feet with no warning," Len shot back. He sat up and reached for a coil of rope. "Now, with that out of the way, I cannot express how long I've been waiting to see you tied up in my bondage instead of someone else's."

Albigard watched with interest and a hint of heat as Len started measuring out hanks of rope.

"I'm going to start with your arms and upper body," he said, talking Albigard through it as he began a diamond pattern for the chest harness and integrated rope columns on both arms to bind them in a crossed position in front of him, pharaoh-style. The tie was intricate, but not overly complex, and took him about twenty minutes to complete.

By the time Len was done, his dick was pressing uncomfortably against the zipper of his jeans, made worse by the fact that he'd chosen to go commando for ease of access when the time came. He stepped back, taking in the picture.

"How's that feel?" he asked.

"Confining," Albigard replied.

"Hmm. Almost as though that's the point," Len told him. "The others are looking at you, you know. Probably wondering what I'm going to do to you now that I've bound you."

A tiny shiver went through Albigard's body. "And what are you going to do to me?"

"Use you for my pleasure, of course," Len said. "That's why you're here, isn't it?" He paused, giving his captive a considering look. "Honestly, you're not nearly helpless enough for my taste yet, but I suppose you can suck me off while I decide how I want you when I'm done tying you up."

The Fae's chin lifted. "What if I don't wish to fellate you?"

Len smiled and stepped into his space, winding the fingers of one hand into his mane of silky hair, and unzipping his fly with the other hand. "What if I don't care?" he retorted, and used his grip to pull Albigard's mouth to him.

Never let it be said that Albigard was a slow learner. Already, his oral skills had improved to a level that meant Len wasn't going to be setting any endurance records tonight. The wet heat, the rasp of a curling tongue, the suction as Len carefully fucked Albigard's mouth—all of it combined to have him coming in two minutes flat. It might have been embarrassing, but embarrassment was the last thing on Len's mind as his pleasure coiled and crested, pulsing his release across Albigard's tongue in heavy spurts.

He let himself feel every exquisite moment, the Fae's throat working as he swallowed around Len's softening cock. Albigard let Len slip free from between his lips, and Len spilled his body backward onto the nest of furs, where his hair formed a tousled halo of palest gold around his head.

"Passable," Len said, striving for indifference. It sounded a bit too breathless to be convincing.

"If I am to be used in such a depraved manner, I might as well strive to gain adequate skill at it," Albigard said, a bit hoarsely, and Len made note of the fact that he was still speaking in full sentences, complete with snark.

Len went straight for the most effective cure for that problem, wrapping a hand around Albigard's impressively hard dick and fisting it with firm strokes. Albigard inhaled sharply and stopped mouthing off.

"You'll be 'used' plenty tonight, not to worry," Len assured him, and let go in favor of reaching for more rope.

He'd positioned the furs near a wall of the grotto that boasted a jutting crag of stone at head height. He used that rock as an anchor point to suspend Albigard's left leg in the air, lifting his hips enough to provide easy access. His right leg,

Len bound with a frog-tie, bent double. When he was satisfied, he went back to jerking Albigard's cock until the Fae began to writhe against the bonds... and discovered that he couldn't move more than a few inches in any direction.

"There. That's much better," Len said, letting him go again.

The Fae's heavy erection fell against his stomach, twitching and leaking from the tip. Albigard breathed raggedly, trying to regain control of himself.

The exposed position gave Len a clearer view of the lower parts of Albigard's tattoo than he'd ever really had before. His earlier impression had been right—while the top spread over the Fae's chest like branches, narrowing to a twisted trunk following the taut line of his abs, the bottom edges curled around the base of Albigard's cock and his balls, spanning his hips and inner thighs to spill onto his glutes, as well. Len traced the organic shapes with a feather-light touch, watching in fascination as they twisted independently, moving beneath his fingertips.

Magic... like so much about the Fae currently on display beneath him.

"Is this tattoo supposed to represent Chaima?" he asked, curiosity overcoming him. He followed the curving black lines over sensitive flesh, feeling the faintest tingles of power through his skin.

Albigard shuddered. "Yes," he rasped.

"Huh," Len said. "As someone famous once said, I guess irony can be pretty ironic sometimes." He gave the twisting roots a final stroke and reached for the simple ball gag he'd brought from Earth. "Anyway, I think that's enough talking. *Open*."

Since Albigard was panting already, it wasn't difficult to slip the rubber ball between his teeth. The Fae's look of comical offense—followed almost immediately by uncertainty as Len buckled the strap around his head and he realized he couldn't spit out the gag—was worth the price of admission all on its own.

"Show me what you're going to do if you need to stop," Len ordered.

Albigard stared at him for a long moment before he let his head fall back in surrender. His fingers flickered, and a little ball of glowing sparkles rose from his hand. A second ball followed a couple of seconds later.

"Well done, princeling," Len said. "Now, it's time for us to have some real fun."

The oil that was available from the same carved shelf as the furs and blankets wasn't anything Len would have recognized as proper lube. But he was also cognizant that this was a guy who refused to wear synthetic fabrics on the grounds that they were too irritating to bear against his skin.

He'd wavered over the bottle of silicone-based lube he'd brought along before deciding that other Fae were probably the best judge of what should go inside a Fae's ass. With condoms not being an issue—since Len had tested clean after his last hookup, and his current partner had been celibate since the time of Charlemagne—Len went with the oil.

Albigard tensed as Len dribbled a copious amount of the stuff between his legs. He added some to his fingers as well and started exploring, while giving a lazy handjob at the same time. The Fae gradually relaxed into the dual sensations as Len teased and circled. By the time he worked a finger far enough inside to confirm the existence of the mythical faerie prostate, Albigard was rolling his hips restlessly, chasing both forms of stimulation.

A muffled moan escaped the gag, and Len's dick began to wake up after his previous orgasm. With a grim smile, Len released Albigard's cock and focused on teasing the walnut-sized bundle of nerves he'd found, while the Fae panted rapidly through his nose.

Danon wandered in as Len was in the process of introducing a second finger. He was one of the people with whom Len had spoken earlier in the evening, and he'd seemed happy enough to act as an unpaid extra in the scene Len had wanted to set. Mostly, he was huge and male and intimidating, but Len trusted him to leave without being offended if the whole thing turned out not to be to Albigard's taste.

The massive Fae came over to the edge of the pool a few feet away from them and started stripping off his clothes. Albigard's green eyes grew very wide indeed.

Danon ran an impassive gaze over Len's rope work, and gestured at the ball gag. "That's a clever little toy," he said. "Finally decided to break this one in good and proper, did you?"

A tremor ran through Albigard's body, and Len felt the hard clench around his fingers. No ball of glowing sparkles sprang from the Fae's hand, though.

"I figured it was time he started earning his keep," Len replied. "Can't be too soft with the prisoners, or they might forget why they're here in the first place."

Danon grunted in agreement and lowered his body into the pool, arranging himself sideways on the stone bench so he could watch the proceedings.

"Anyway," Len continued, "the line forms on the left." He paused. "Do you like men? I should've asked earlier."

"Eh, I prefer women, but I'm not picky," Danon said. "A fair number of the pretty boys who end up here are in desperate need of a good reaming."

"Right?" Len agreed, and twisted his wrist. "I told this one the same thing. I said, any time when you aren't getting fucked is a tragic waste." He gestured at Albigard's bound body with his free hand. "I mean, look at him. If he's not filled at both ends and covered in his own come, what's the point of even having him here?"

Albigard made a ragged, desperate noise around the gag. His cock twitched and jumped as Len crooked his fingers, attacking his prostate with renewed determination.

"He looks like one that could go all night, it's true," Danon observed.

Len pulled out and dribbled more oil on his hand before adding a third finger. "The virginal ones are always the most fun," he said, searching out the perfect angle again. "They look so surprised when they realize how much they love taking it up the ass."

A muffled cry slipped past the gag as Albigard arched, his cock pulsing in strong spurts as he came untouched. Len kept milking him until he was a shuddering mess... and longer still, until he was whimpering and writhing, trying to get away, but with nowhere to go.

"Well," Danon observed in a clinical tone, "he's definitely covered in his own come now, so you're halfway there." He stretched, making a production of it. "Maybe I'll go round up some of the lads while you finish giving him his first ride."

"You do that." Len backed off Albigard's prostate and ran his free hand through the mess on his stomach, smearing it around. He watched, fascinated, as the tattoo of Chaima writhed once more beneath his touch, the roots and branches curling against Albigard's pale skin. "After all, we've got the whole night."

Albigard let out an unsteady breath.

Len continued stroking and scissoring him open as Danon hauled himself out of the water and dried off. The huge Fae dressed and headed out with a small, ironic salute in Len's direction. The handful of others who'd been present when Albigard had first arrived had also left, heading for their bedrolls as midnight approached.

"Looks like it's just you and me now, princeling," Len said, gentling his movements as Albigard slowly turned to jelly beneath his hands. "Good thing I had you suck me off earlier, since it means I'll last long enough now to give you the fucking you truly deserve."

The liquid gaze that blinked up at him was its own consent—hazy pleasure shot through with wanting. Something low in Len's stomach tightened at the sight. He slid his fingers free and washed his hands in the pool, using the bar of Irish Spring soap he'd bought for the trip... because even if no one here got the joke, it was still *hilarious*, thank you very much.

When he was done, he knelt beside Albigard and unbuckled the gag, sliding it out of his mouth. Albigard worked his jaw for a moment before settling back, still half-gone.

"It's time. Beg me for it, princeling," Len said in a gentle tone.

"Please," Albigard replied, without hesitation.

"Please, what?" Len prompted.

"Please take me now. I don't want the others. I only want you."

Len had to close his eyes for a moment. "Then you'll only have me," he managed. "After hearing you say that, I'm not inclined to share."

Hands feeling none too steady, Len opened his fly and oiled his erection, kneeling over Albigard on the furs as he lined himself up. Albigard was loose and pliant beneath him, what remained of his body's defenses giving way with remarkable ease as Len pushed in. He stilled, wanting to give his partner time to get used to the new sensation... but Albigard's hips curled greedily, taking him all the way.

The Fae gasped, and Len bit the inside of his cheek to hold back the surge of pleasure as tight heat enveloped him. Slowly, tentatively, they built a rhythm together. Len hooked an elbow behind the knee of the leg that was tied to the rock above them, using the leverage to bend Albigard's spine until he could reach the Fae's lips.

They kissed, hips rolling to meet with every slow thrust, until Len felt Albigard begin to harden against his stomach. He kept up the easy rhythm until it all started to become too much. When he knew he wouldn't be able to be hold back much longer, Len broke the kiss and knelt back, wrapping a hand around Albigard's cock and jerking him in time with his increasingly sloppy thrusts.

The Fae went rigid, muscles locked, and his body clamped around Len's as he came. Len was right there with him, his entire world narrowing down to the place where they were joined as his release hit him in a series of almost painful spasms.

"Jesus... *god*," he cursed, gasping as his vision wavered back into focus.

Albigard was breathing heavily beneath him, and they lay in a tangle for a few moments until Len managed to reconnect his brain to his muscles. He slipped out as carefully as he could, and contemplated the intricate shibari tie for approximately two seconds before reaching for the knife he'd kept within easy reach. It took only moments to cut Albigard loose.

Len looked regretfully at the ruined rope when he was done. This was why actual shibari *sex* was something of a pain in the ass. No one wanted to untie dozens of knots right after they'd come as hard as Len just had. He tossed the unraveling pieces of rope aside and peeled off his jeans.

"Come here, princeling," he said. "We're washing off now, before your muscles seize up and the jizz dries on our stomachs."

Albigard made a blissed out, noncommittal noise, but allowed himself to be manhandled into the nearby pool. Len slipped an arm around his shoulders and propped the Fae's head against the crook of his neck, since he sensed that drowning avoidance tactics weren't hugely high on Albigard's priority list right now. He cleaned them both up as best he could. Afterward, they soaked until Len's already relaxed muscles were in danger of melting completely, and then crawled out of the pool to collapse onto the nest of furs and blankets.

Len claimed the role of big spoon, fitting his body behind Albigard's and pressing close. The Fae made a noise of utter contentment as Len brushed his lips against the nape of his neck.

"Love you," Len whispered against his skin — not really having intended to say the words aloud, but not regretting them, either.

Albigard gave a sleepy hum. "Do you frequently express amorous emotions to the orangutans at the zoo?" he murmured.

A smile curved Len's lips, as a bright bubble of amusement burst in his chest. "Not frequently, no," he said.

"Nor I," Albigard agreed. "It takes a very exceptional orangutan indeed."

"Hmm," Len said, and yawned. "Well, let me know if you ever come across such an unusual specimen."

Albigard settled closer and covered Len's arm with his.

"I believe I just did," the Fae replied.

finis

Nigellus' story begins in *The Sixth Demon: Book One.*

To discover more books by this author, visit
www.rasteffan.com

Made in the USA
Coppell, TX
29 January 2022